RINK RIVALS

Also by Jacqueline Guest
in the Lorimer Sports Stories series:

Free Throw
A Goal in Sight
Hat Trick
Rookie Season
Soccer Star
Triple Threat

RINK RIVALS

Jacqueline Guest

James Lorimer & Company Ltd., Publishers
Toronto

James Lorimer & Company Ltd., Publishers acknowledges the support of the Ontario Arts Council. We acknowledge the financial support of the Government of Canada through the Canada Book Fund for our publishing activities. We acknowledge the support of the Canada Council for the Arts for our publishing program. We acknowledge the Government of Ontario through the Ontario Media Development Corporation's Ontario Book Initiative.

Cover design: Meredith Bangay

Library and Archives Canada Cataloguing in Publication

Guest, Jacqueline
Rink rivals / by Jacqueline Guest.

(Sports stories)
Issued also in an electronic format.
ISBN 978-1-55277-565-3

I. Title. II. Series: Sports stories (Toronto, Ont.)

PS8563.U365R55 2010 jC813'.54 C2010-903312-4

James Lorimer & Company Ltd., Publishers
317 Adelaide Street West, Suite 1002
Toronto, ON, Canada
M5V 1P9
www.lorimer.ca

Distributed in the United States by:
Orca Book Publishers
P.O. Box 468
Custer, WA USA
98240-0468

Printed and bound in Canada
Manufactured by Friesens Corporation in Altona, Manitoba, Canada in August 2010.
Job # 58189

CONTENTS

For Colleen,
I count myself lucky because I can call you my friend. Thanks for being the best support system a writer ever had!

1 THE CHALLENGE

The roar of the huge aircraft's jet engines filled the air as it began the final approach to the runway. Thirteen-year-old twin brothers Evan and Brynley Selkirk exchanged looks. They were finally arriving in Calgary, Alberta after a long and exhausting flight.

Evan sat next to his mother, Julianne. She reached over and pushed his lanky hair out of his hazelnut brown eyes in a familiar gesture which she'd made since he was a small boy. "We made it." She smiled at her son and patted his hair down.

Evan frowned at his mom for the babyish gesture. His mom, who was a James Bay Cree, had dark brown hair like his, but hers was thick and shiny and looked great, while his just seemed to hang limply straight down, usually into his eyes, which was why his mom was always fussing with it. His skin was dark like hers, but where she was short and fine-boned, he was built more like his dad—tall and sturdy.

It was because of his mom that they were moving

from their home in the tiny isolated community of Whapmagoostui, Quebec. She was a lawyer and had accepted a new job with a top-notch firm here in Calgary. Whapmagoostui, on the east coast of Hudson Bay, was a very long way from Calgary.

As the plane broke through the clouds, Evan looked out the window at the tiny houses flashing by below. Calgary, situated where the prairie meets the mountains, was surrounded by a colourful patchwork of flat farm fields to the east and rolling foothills climbing up the shoulders of the Rockies to the west.

Occasional drifts of gleaming snow reminded Evan it was early November and winter, even this far south. The gently rolling prairie stretching off into the distance was quite a change from the endless grey, frigid waters of Hudson Bay. And here, he noticed, there were roads absolutely everywhere.

Back home, they had few roads because there were very few cars to use them. In the summer, people drove quads—small, four-wheeled, all-terrain vehicles—and in the winter everyone used snowmobiles.

Evan looked past his mother to his brother, Bryn. Blonde with ice-blue eyes and a fine bone structure, Evan's brother looked like a poster boy for Angels Anonymous. He and his brother had never gotten along and seldom saw eye-to-eye on anything. It wasn't Evan's fault; he was the normal one. For instance, Evan lived for hockey, which was completely cool for a thirteen-year-old guy, whereas his wimpy brother Bryn didn't play hockey. In fact, Bryn didn't do any sports; instead, he played the piano—*a lot*.

Just then, Bryn glanced up from his book and caught Evan looking at him. He gave Evan a dirty look.

Evan ignored his brother, pretending instead to be looking at his dad, Thomas, who was sitting in the next bank of seats. His dad, who was usually neat and precise in his appearance, was now distinctly rumpled after the tiring flight. His shirt was creased and his curly blonde hair looked as if he'd just climbed out of bed. There were dark smudges under his pale blue eyes. He had been the only white elementary school teacher in Whapmagoostui and had been well-liked by his students.

Stuck in the aisle seat, Bryn had to lean forward to peer out the small window for his first glimpse of their new home. "Look at the size of this place!" he exclaimed when he saw the rows upon rows of houses. His eyes were shining. "Calgary's so big, I bet they have their own philharmonic orchestra."

Evan rolled his eyes. He knew his brother loved music. It was probably because for as long as Evan could remember, Bryn had songs playing in his head, like background music in a movie. In Evan's books, this made Bryn a freak because of the way he was always tuned in. His brother said his brain and body seemed to work faster with his private music playing.

Bryn started to bob his head up and down and Evan knew he was listening to his head music. It was probably a boring piano piece. Bryn planned on being a classical pianist when he grew up and would torture Evan by practising for hours.

The two boys gave each other one last glare, then sat back in their seats and waited for the long journey from their old home to end. The plane touched down with a gentle bump.

Their new adventure was about to begin.

★★★

The weekend was spent moving into their house and arranging for the boys' new school.

Slouching against the doorjamb of his brother's new room, Evan watched Bryn struggle with a large poster. "You're not going to put those stupid things up, are you?" he asked, folding his arms and nodding at the stack of posters waiting on Bryn's bed.

His brother scowled. "I'll put up whatever I like in my room." He nodded toward the pile of posters, which held portraits of such famous composers as Mozart, Pachelbel, and Chopin. "These geniuses have stood the test of time and come out on top." He finished hanging the large poster. "Ludwig van B., here," he jerked his thumb at the picture of Beethoven, "happens to be my hero."

Evan scoffed. "Yeah, right. Only someone with no

life would think that. If you ever want to fit in with big-city people, you'll have to try acting normal, and that means changing your artwork for a start."

"Like you got voted Mr. Popularity at our old school. If the kids had taken a vote, I know you'd have been chosen *Boy Most Likely To End Up Alone On Some Deserted Island By Choice.* Besides, look who's giving out advice on fitting in with normal people, *Mr. Stamp Album*!" Bryn laughed and reached for another poster. This one was of George Frederick Handel.

Evan's face burned. Up north there hadn't been a lot to do besides hang out or scream around on your quad or snowmobile. Stamp collecting, his secret hobby, had let him escape the boredom by imagining all the far-off places depicted on the stamps.

He would order packages over the Internet and wait patiently for them to arrive. Then he'd use the family computer to research each stamp's country until he knew everything he could about the exotic, far-off land. He'd never told anyone at his old school about his stamps. They wouldn't have understood.

Glaring at Bryn, Evan turned and went back to his room which had absolutely nothing on the walls, except for one small framed picture of a blindfolded woman with a sword in one hand and holding a pair of balancing scales in the other.

★★★

The boys were surprised when their mother and father called them into the living room. They sat quietly while their dad paced up and down as though he were about to lecture his grade eight science class on photosynthesis.

"I realize as twins," he began, "that you two have always been together in school. I don't think it's a hard and fast rule that you remain together in your education. Your mother and I have come up with an unusual plan."

He nodded at Bryn. "Bryn, you'll be going to Westhaven Academy. It's a well-respected school with a reputation for its fine musical program. Your mother and I both think you'll do well there. In fact, with your talent, you may be qualified for their Musical Protégé Program, which would get you the best tutors and a chance for a musical scholarship. You'd have to keep a B+ average in your academic work, but it's all there for you, Bryn."

He turned to his other son. "Evan, because you plan a career in the law," his father smiled at him, "you'll be attending Turner Middle School, known for its very high academic standards. Fortunately, you've never had too much trouble with marks. We've checked out both institutions and think that, although it means sending you to two different schools, it would be a great opportunity for you both."

For once, Evan and Bryn sat speechless.

Evan was the first to respond. "I won't have to go to the same school as the music freak? This is going to be great!"

Bryn ignored his brother. "A school just for kids who like music?" he asked excitedly. "All right!"

"It's not just music, Bryn," his father went on. "Westhaven has a sound academic program as well as an active athletic department. It will give you a chance to try new things. We were told some Westhaven students play on a minor league hockey team." He smiled hopefully at his son.

"Yeah, right," Evan snickered, thinking of his brother's aversion to anything involving team sports and sweat.

Their dad continued, ignoring the boy's shot at his brother. "I checked out Turner Middle School and a lot of their students play league hockey also." He smiled at Evan. "You could talk to them. They might know of a team that could use an eager new starter like yourself."

Evan thought about this. Up north they had a long season and he had always been on the local team. He was a forward and had been a number-one player. Hockey was the only place Evan felt he really fit in. He'd always kept to himself because the other kids got on his nerves. He found them annoying and dumb. His mom said it was because he was "gifted" and "very bright," so perhaps his classmates couldn't get the answers as fast as he did. He'd never felt comfortable with the rest of the students in Whapmagoostui.

Evan wondered if this school would be different. His dad had said they had high academic standards, and that meant kids who could handle learning new ideas faster. Maybe he'd actually like these kids and perhaps they'd like him. He would never say it, but sometimes the idea of being popular seemed cool to him. He'd check the place out and who knows, maybe join the local team, be a hero, a winner, fit in. If he played his usual star-level hockey and pulled down A's...

Bryn's words cut in on Evan's thoughts. "That's just what this hockey hero needs!" he said. "A school that's as sports nuts as he is."

Evan was instantly annoyed. "It takes a lot to play good hockey, jerk. It's not just skating around with a piece of lumber in your hands. Just because you wouldn't know how to tie your own skates without help..."

Bryn scoffed at the old argument. "Oh yeah? Like I couldn't play hockey if I wanted to! You don't have to be some sort of superman to hit a puck and I know I can skate nearly as well as you!" Brynley's face flushed at what they all knew was a huge exaggeration. He could skate, but nothing like his brother.

Evan snorted. "Why don't you put your skates where your mouth is, Music Boy? You heard Dad. Some Westhaven kids play on a league team. I doubt you could." Evan stood very close to Bryn, poking his finger into his brother's chest. *"I bet there's no way you can make the hockey grade."*

Bryn shoved Evan's hand away angrily.

"You're on, Brainiac!" Bryn said confidently.

"Maybe that will shut you up, once and for all. Oh, and by the way, you do know you have to at least talk to the rest of your team to play. If I remember correctly, being social with anyone has always been a problem for you. *I bet I'm on a team before you even get an audition!*"

"An *audition*? Ha!" Evan laughed sarcastically. "You mean a *tryout,* you loser."

"That's enough, boys!" Their mother's quiet, authoritative voice cut them off. "I think it's a great idea for you *both* to play hockey. The competition would be exciting. It would also be a great way to meet and make new friends." She looked at her husband. "What do you think, Thomas? Can we chauffeur two hockey stars around for a season?"

Their dad smiled at them as if this was a dream come true. He'd always wanted the boys to play. His smile signalled his approval. "I think that could be arranged."

Neither Evan nor Bryn said another word. Instead, they glared at each other.

2 NEW SCHOOL BLUES

The first day at a new school is always the worst, and Bryn's beginning at Westhaven Academy was no different. It felt as if the other kids were staring at him, as though he had two heads and one of them was screwed on backwards. Bryn hated feeling like he didn't belong. He'd always been okay with the kids at his old school, but he'd grown up with them. These big city kids with their expensive clothes and sophisticated mannerisms made him feel like a real hick from the sticks. He'd thought because he loved music, he'd feel right at home here, but he felt like an alien from another planet.

Bryn sat outside the vice-principal's office and waited. The clock on the wall ticked so loudly it intruded on a particularly cool song that was humming through his head.

"Master Selkirk!" a voice boomed, cutting through the closing verse of the song.

Startled, Bryn jumped up, hastily straightening the new blue and red school necktie he'd put on with such difficulty that morning. It was weird wearing a uniform. The only time he got decked out was to go to church, but here he was in his brilliant white shirt, too-tight tie, itchy grey trousers, and a stiff navy blazer complete with a crest on the pocket. He turned, looking into the stern face of the vice-principal.

"Yes...sir," Bryn said, forgetting the elderly man's name.

"It's *Mister Boothby* to my friends." He had a strong British accent. There wasn't a flicker of a smile on his well-wrinkled face, but his tone had softened and there was a merry glint in his faded grey eyes.

Bryn warmed to the old white-haired teacher instantly. He looked like one of the Cree elders from back home.

"This is Miss Coles." The ancient teacher motioned to a student about Bryn's age who flashed him a brilliant smile. "She'll be your *study buddy*!" He pronounced each syllable very precisely. "We've found this system works well with new students while they're getting used to our methods here at Westhaven." He nodded at Bryn and the pretty girl. "Now off you go. You're expected in your first class in five minutes."

"It's Kelsey," the girl whispered as the two hurriedly left.

Bryn glanced over at her. Her thick, curly brown hair was drawn up on either side of her head and fastened with pink elastic devices Bryn decided came under the heading of *girl stuff.* He noticed her deep brown eyes twinkled mischievously. He knew it was rude to stare, but he couldn't help himself. She was really cute, and he wasn't a guy who used the word often, if at all.

"And it's okay to get closer. I don't bite," she said, as he continued to gawk speechlessly at her.

In addition to her glossy brown hair and sparkling dark eyes, Kelsey Coles was skinny and nearly as tall as he was. She had rather large front teeth, but somehow they added character to her face. When you put the whole thing together, it worked great, Bryn decided, as he smiled shyly back. He wasn't sure what to say. For some reason, she made him feel nervous.

"My name's Bryn...Bryn Selkirk. But you know my name is Selkirk because Mr. Boothby introduced us," he stammered. He could feel his face redden and this made him even more self-conscious. He knew he was babbling, but couldn't seem to shut up. "I'm new here, but you know that too or you wouldn't be with me." He was out of control now. His tie seemed to be strangling him and he could feel sweat starting to bead up on his forehead.

Kelsey stopped and looked at him. "Relax! You're blabbing like a geek and I'm sure you're not."

Bryn took a deep breath. He did his best to relax.

Then he looked at her again and felt his stomach whirl around like it was in a blender.

"I'm part of the Study Buddy Program. When a new student enrols, they're paired up with someone from the program. It's just until you know your way around." She smiled brightly at him and he swallowed.

She went on. "There's a list and we take turns with the new students. I guess it was your lucky day, Bryn Selkirk, because my name was next on the list." She shouldered her way through the hallways like a seasoned fullback.

Bryn nodded in mute agreement. He suddenly felt at ease with this outgoing tour guide. Maybe Westhaven wasn't going to be so bad after all.

★★★

The rest of the day flew by. Kelsey walked him to each of his classes letting him in on any gossip about the teacher or students in that particular room. She seemed to know an incredible amount about what went on in Westhaven.

"How do you know all this stuff?" Bryn asked as they were walking toward his last class of the day.

"Oh, I keep my eyes open and I hear things. I'm a very good listener," she explained. "And it doesn't hurt when your dad is on the faculty."

"Your dad teaches here?" Bryn asked.

"He teaches phys. ed. and he also coaches the world's best hockey team, the Comets. My brother Lucas is the captain." He could hear the pride in her voice. "In fact, there's a practice today. I'm heading over to the rink right after school. I think hockey players are *so* cool, don't you?" she asked.

"Hockey, great!" Bryn said excitedly thinking of his bet with his brother. "Hey, if you wouldn't mind I'd really be interested in watching the practice. Can I come with you?" He looked at her hopefully. This was too good to be true. First day at school and he was going to meet the coach and the captain of the Comets! At this rate his brother was in for a big surprise tonight at dinner.

"Sure, I'd love the company and practice is always interesting. Do you play?" she asked, waiting on his reply.

He looked at Kelsey. Being with her wouldn't be too tough to handle either, he decided. He suddenly realized he wanted to play hockey for the Comets very much. Not just because of Evan; the idea of doing something Kelsey so obviously thought was great was very appealing, too.

"Me, play hockey? Ah, well, yeah sure, I can play. I was on the ice with the team at my old school in Whapmagoostui." This was true, sort of. The fact that he had just been skating while the hockey team practised on the other half of the rink was beside the point.

Even though he hadn't actually played, he'd seen enough hockey, he was sure he could. After being dragged to what seemed like hundreds of his brother's games, he knew every detail of the sport and could recall all the moves Evan was famous for.

The warm smile Kelsey beamed at him made all his misgivings disappear. Just then several noisy kids in band uniforms walked by laughing and talking.

"Oh, brother! Will you get a load of those hats!" she whispered as the musicians moved past them. "Band geeks! They really are unbelievable. Who in their right mind would want to waste their lives running around carrying a tuba wearing that getup, all in the name of music?" She laughed.

Suddenly Bryn felt a little strange. He was a musician. He had an appointment with the music instructor tomorrow after school to plan his piano schedule! His first goal was to get on the Protégé Program. Music was why he was at Westhaven. But if she felt like this about the band...He would have to tell Kelsey about his music, but maybe the actual *telling* part could wait until she knew him better and perhaps liked him a little more.

He nodded his head hesitantly and laughed. "Yeah, I've never been much for tuba solos myself either." He thought his laugh sounded totally phoney.

She stopped in front of his classroom door. "I'll meet you later and we can go to the arena." She gave him one more dazzling smile, then headed down the hallway.

Bryn watched her go. He was going to talk to a coach about playing hockey. He could do this. He *would* do this. And for the record, Kelsey Coles was awesome!

***

As promised, Kelsey was waiting for him after class. Together, they headed to the sports arena that was adjacent to the school. A cold November breeze had sprung up and they were wearing warm jackets, hats, and mitts to ward off the chill. Bryn noticed how the nip in the breeze made Kelsey's cheeks turn bright pink and the way her dark curls peeked out from under her woollen cap.

"I told Lucas you were coming," she said, turning her collar up so it framed her small face. "He's looking forward to swapping plays with you."

Kelsey had stepped out onto the street to cross when Bryn noticed a beat up old van pull around the corner and head right for them. He reached out and grabbed Kelsey's coat, yanking her back onto the sidewalk.

"Careful!" he shouted as the van sped past, narrowly missing them both.

"Whew!" Kelsey gasped as she watched the noisy vehicle drive away. "I know those guys. They're from the First Nations reserve outside of town." She straightened her coat and started across the street again. "My dad's right about that kind. They are a big waste of space."

Shocked at her attitude, Bryn tried not to look at her.

"Hey, you saved me! You're my hero!" Kelsey giggled. The gratitude in her voice made him blush.

"It was nothing, honest," he said modestly. He looked down at his shoes, noticing the shine had gone from the polish he'd given them this morning.

He felt confused. Kelsey was the best thing that had happened to him in a long time, but some of the things she said were difficult for him to take. The comment on musicians was bad enough, but what she said about the Indian kids in the van—that was brutal. His mom was one of the best, most honest, smartest, hardest-working people he knew and she was Cree! He was very proud of his mom. His being half Cree had never been an issue before. Up north, most people were a mix of white and Cree, or Innu and Cree, or just plain Cree, or any number of combinations. On the west side of Hudson Bay there were the Inuit who spoke Inuktitut, which added to the northern mix of people. Up there, people were just people first. After that they were smart or not so smart, good or bad, then, if there was nothing else cool about them, Indian or white.

But if he was going to get on the hockey team, and he wanted to now more than ever, he had better hide that part of his life, along with his music. He decided he wouldn't keep it a secret forever, just until Kelsey saw what a great guy he was, even if he did play the piano and was half Cree. He didn't say anything more as they made their way to the arena.

★★★

Kelsey and Bryn sat in the spectator's area and waited while the players on the ice ran through their drills. When a stop in the action sent the players for a break, Bryn and Kelsey headed down to the bench.

After the introductions were made, Kelsey excitedly explained how Bryn had saved her from being run over "by those losers from the reserve."

"Bryn grabbed my coat and with a show of amazing strength, pulled me out of harm's way." She nodded her head as she spoke. "He's a teenaged superhero," she added, smiling at Bryn who felt embarrassed under the onslaught of her glowing praise.

"I'd like to thank you, Bryn," Coach Coles said. "It was a good thing you were there."

"I know she can be a pain in the butt, but she's the only sister I have. Thanks. I'm Lucas, in case my fame hasn't reached you yet." He smiled at Bryn. "But if you've been hanging out with my sister, you've probably had an earful already. Kelsey's my biggest fan." He ruffled his sister's curly hair.

"Bryn wants to play for the Comets," Kelsey said, shoving her brother's hand away.

"We can always use talent," Coach Coles smiled at Bryn. "I've got some spare skates. Would you like to show us what you can do?"

Bryn felt cornered. Now what? The minute he hit the ice, they were going to know he couldn't really play. He'd look like an idiot in front of Kelsey.

"Well, actually, that may not be...I have my school uniform on..." Bryn began feebly.

"Sure he will!" Kelsey volunteered. "Don't worry about your clothes. It's just a skate, Bryn, nothing serious." She turned an enthusiastic face to him. "This is going to be great!"

He knew he had no choice. "You bet!" he said weakly, forcing a smile. "Where are those skates, Coach?" He didn't mind having to try out. It was doing it in front of Kelsey that made him nervous. He laced the skates up and took the hockey stick Lucas offered.

"I'll introduce you to some of the team," Lucas said. "We'll do some drills, then you can try and get one past our goalie." He nodded toward the net. "But I warn you, Jordan is wicked between the pipes."

"Great..." Bryn hefted the unfamiliar stick as he followed the energetic young captain.

"Guys," Lucas said calling the skaters together. "This is Bryn Selkirk and he wants to be a Comet. I play centre and this is Tyler McBride, left forward. Sean Fowler is the other winger and Zach Lansky, right defence. Over there is Aaron Bard, who thinks he can play left defence. And this," he patted the goalie on top of his helmet. "Is the best darn goalie in the league, Jordan Cairn."

Bryn noticed the goalie was very short and had a slight build. He wondered how Jordan stood up against some of the bigger players when they fired slapshots at him.

"We can always use another good player," Tyler added.

"Yeah, Lucas needs all the help he can get," Jordan laughed.

The next fifteen minutes would have made top ratings on the Hockey Hall of Fame Bloopers. Bryn zigged when he should have zagged, nearly running Aaron into the boards. He overshot a great pass from Zach, then fell turning to pick up the puck. He crashed straight into Lucas, sending them both sprawling in a tangle of sticks and skates. During his short skate, he rammed himself into the boards so many times he felt bruised all over although no one had laid a glove on him.

At one point, Bryn had skated toward the net and fired, then noticed Jordan was taking a drink. It would have been a cheap goal if it had gone in, but the puck sailed wide of the crease and hit the boards.

Bryn winced. He was praying the humiliating experience would end when Lucas skated over to him.

"I'm guessing you don't really have a lot of experience with league play?" he asked. "Or maybe *any* play?" He gave Bryn a knowing look.

Bryn looked a little sheepish. "It was a very small league," he said, not looking at Lucas.

"It doesn't matter. Hockey should be fun too. How about we pepper Jordan with a couple of hotshot plays?"

"Sounds good to me," Bryn agreed, groaning inwardly.

"Okay, we'll start from the blue line and pass back and forth. I'll cut left; you pass me the puck and head for the slot. I'll tip it back and you slam it home." Lucas headed toward the blue line.

Bryn followed. He swallowed nervously, feeling panic rising inside him. He didn't know what to do to stop the out-of-control wave of doom.

Suddenly an old rock and roll tune he'd had running in his head earlier that day popped back into his mind at full volume. He couldn't shut it out.

He began skating, picking up speed as he listened to the beat in his head. Effortlessly, he dodged around the other players. They laughed at the new guy and tried to stop his advance. Bryn was able to avoid them without even knowing how he was doing it. The music kept on playing and Bryn felt himself moving to the beat. He could see Lucas start his run to the left. Bryn deked right, then cut hard to the slot in time to connect perfectly with Lucas's pass. He swung his stick and, as the music hit a climax, smacked the puck as hard as he could.

Jordan was so surprised, he left the five-hole open between his skates and the puck sailed straight through.

"All right, Bryn!" Kelsey cheered from the penalty box where she was watching.

"Nice shooting," Lucas said patting Bryn on the helmet.

The other players waved sticks and gloved hands.

Bryn and Lucas skated to the bench.

"What do you say, Dad, is he on the Comets?" Kelsey asked as soon as the two skaters came off the ice.

Coach Coles looked hesitant. "It's a little late in the season to bring a rookie in, honey."

Bryn looked down at his skates. He knew the coach was thinking about the crash and bash style of hockey he'd demonstrated so well. Sure he'd managed one goal, but that was a fluke. He didn't blame the coach.

"Daddy, he did rescue me from what could have been a fatal accident…" Kelsey looked up at her dad with expressive brown eyes. "Lucas will work with him until he's up to speed as a Comet."

"Does the captain get any say in this?" Lucas asked.

"Only if you agree with me that Bryn should be given a chance on the Comets." Kelsey shot her brother a warning look.

Bryn cleared his throat. "It's okay, Kelsey. I understand. Maybe next year."

Lucas punched him on the shoulder, making Bryn wince. "What's the matter? You don't want me to teach you? I'm not good enough?"

"Oh, no, it's not that," Bryn said quickly. "That would be great, if it's not too much trouble. If I get on the team, I mean."

All three kids looked at Coach Coles who seemed to be thinking things over.

"You're a little weak on a few details," the coach

said, nodding slowly, "but if you can shoot like that last goal in a game, you'll do okay. If Lucas is willing to work with you, I guess there's no reason we can't give it a try. There's a spot on the Comet lineup if you want one, Bryn." He laid his hand on Bryn's shoulder and smiled. "But it may not be in the starting lineup."

Bryn thought about the offer. If he took the position, he'd be committed. He'd have to practise and play. He'd never been athletic, what made him think he could pull this off? He began having cold feet, and not from standing on the ice. Then he looked at Kelsey's face. How could he say no to her?

"I'd be proud to play for the Comets." He nodded at the coach.

"Then it's settled," Kelsey said with a grin. "Do we have a numbered jersey he could use, Lucas?" Kelsey asked her brother, eyeing Bryn for size.

"Number sixteen is available. We could have your name put on it later." Lucas offered.

Bryn thought for a moment. "Sixteen just became my lucky number," he smiled. He didn't care if his name was on it or not. It would be his first team uniform and he would wear it proudly.

Kelsey looked at her brother. "When's number sixteen's first extra practice, Lucas?"

"How about tomorrow after school?" Lucas asked.

"That's okay with me. I'll bring my equipment to school and meet you here." Bryn was hoping he could round up enough old equipment of Evan's to look like he played.

Winning the bet with his brother had been easier than he expected. Living up to the consequences was going to be tricky.

3 THE NIGHTHAWKS

Evan was apprehensive as he pulled on his skates at the Lakeview Rink. His first day at Turner Middle School hadn't gone well. The kids had turned out to have real working brains, but after so many years of being a loner, he found it hard to make the small talk required to get to know his new classmates.

He was surprised by how much he actually wanted to fit in. It was a new feeling for him. He brushed his hair out of his eyes before pulling on his helmet. He had never cared what his loser classmates had thought of him before or felt the need for friends. But now, he discovered, it was suddenly important to him not to be the kid on the outside looking in.

At lunch earlier that day, he'd been standing in line at the cafeteria when he'd overheard two boys talking.

"Yeah, Stokes is out. He broke his leg when he tried checking that Cougar defenceman into the goalpost. Man, it was messy." The boy speaking was Trevor Wells and the other Jamie Carver. Evan had seen them in his class earlier. He knew they played on the Nighthawks, the team that was currently in first place in the standings. He moved a little closer so he could hear what they were saying better.

"It's going to leave us short a good forward," Jamie answered with a shake of his crazy curly hair.

Evan thought quickly. Here was the golden opportunity he'd been wanting. Hockey was very big at Turner and it was something he understood. He felt comfortable around hockey. If he wanted to run with the in crowd, playing for the hottest team going would be a great start.

He moved up behind the two hockey players.

"I can fill in for your missing forward," he said casually.

Both players turned to look at him suspiciously.

"Who invited you to join this conversation?" Jamie asked, narrowing his eyes.

"I don't think you understand what we need," Trevor said with a superior tone.

He had a scar across the bridge of his nose. Probably from fighting on the ice, Evan thought. "I know how to play killer hockey," he said coolly. "And I need a team to play for."

"You'd have to do more than talk tough," Jamie said sarcastically. "Besides, the man you need to talk to is sitting over there." He indicated a tough looking, dark-haired boy. "That's Craig Carpenter, the team captain. If you want to play, he has the final say."

"Then that's the guy I'll talk to. Thanks," Evan said with a nod of his head as he started toward where the boy sat.

"I hear you're looking for a good forward."

The captain of the Nighthawks looked up from his lunch and fixed him with icy eyes. "Maybe," he said in a low voice. "Who wants to know?"

"My name is Evan Selkirk and I'm new at Turner. The important thing is I can play hockey and you're looking for a replacement for your wounded forward. I'd say you need me as much as I need you." He waited for the boy's response.

Craig shoved his empty lunch tray away. "You're some kind of Indian, aren't you?" he asked, noticing Evan's dark hair and skin.

Evan was momentarily taken aback. "Yeah, *some kind*. My mom's Cree and she's from James Bay. My dad's white and from New Brunswick, so what?" His voice had become defensive.

"I heard Indian kids play rough hockey." He looked at Evan suspiciously.

"If you want to win, you play tough hockey, and there's a difference. To be a great player, whether you're Indian or white or green or purple, you've got to be able to take it as well as dish it out." Evan wasn't sure he liked the way this conversation was going.

"You've got a really pushy attitude problem, Selkirk."

Craig's mouth was set in a hard line.

Evan swallowed. He may have just blown his one chance to get on the Nighthawks.

A smile slowly spread across the team captain's face. "I like that in a teammate. Show up at Lakeview Rink at five o'clock and we'll see what you can do. And Selkirk," his eyes looked like pieces of flint, "you'd better be as good as advertised."

Afterwards, Evan had left the cafeteria feeling more excited than he had in a long time, but that was at lunch—now he had to prove he could back up what he'd said.

His dad had been enthusiastic when he drove Evan to the rink. "Show them some of your moves, Evan. You're the best darn player this side of Whapmagoostui. I know that will impress these big-city boys," he'd said with a wink, then left for the stands.

Taking a deep breath, Evan hit the ice with a rush. He enjoyed the feel of his blades cutting through the slick surface. He noticed right away the ice felt different, smooth as glass. He'd been told it was because they used soft water. These guys down south had it all.

After a couple of warm-up laps, Evan felt ready to take on their best squad. He wanted this and, he decided grimly, he was willing to do whatever it took to get it.

The Nighthawks were a tough-looking team and all the players were big. Craig played right forward,

Trevor at centre, with Jamie right defence, and a huge bruiser named Tank Gowan was the other defenceman. A mean-looking guy in a goalie's uniform was introduced as Paco Jenkins.

Grinning, the teammates lined up at centre ice. Paco, waiting in the crease far behind the other players, slapped his pads with his stick.

"The object of the game is to get this," Craig tossed a puck onto the ice, "by *us.*" His mouth twisted in a peculiar sneer, "And into the net, Selkirk."

Evan nodded. "No sweat."

He began moving forward, his skates churning faster and faster. He felt like he was floating just above the ice. Letting his natural reflexes guide him, he cut left as Trevor moved up to meet him. With a quick dodge he skated between Craig and Jamie, looping behind as he drove toward the net.

Craig, recovering from this dodge, had spun around and moved in to block Evan's advance to the net.

Evan tensed his muscles, lowered himself a little over his skates and hit Craig hard.

The Nighthawks captain had not anticipated the force of the check and momentarily lost his balance.

Evan skated past him without a second look. He was totally focused.

Paco was ready for him. He had moved far out of the net as Evan skated alone across the blue line. As Evan's attack closed in, the goalie glided smoothly back into the crease, cutting down the angles. He used the butterfly style of netminding, but this was nothing new to Evan.

Evan moved in and, starting an impressive looking windup, badly faked a shot to the lower left corner. Paco, anticipating the fake, ignored the shot. Evan flipped the puck to his backhand and again faked a low shot. This one looked real and Paco went for it, dropping to his knees. Evan quickly pulled the puck in close and with a lightning shot slammed it over the goalie into the upper right-hand corner of the net. Paco's glove came up, but it was too little, too late. The puck buried itself in the back of the net.

"Nice check, Selkirk," Craig said, rubbing his shoulder as he skated up behind Evan. "You're stronger than you look. How do you feel about using that muscle on the ice for the Nighthawks?"

Evan had never played as an enforcer before. He had always used his brain when on the ice and didn't like dirty plays, but he wanted to be on the Nighthawks and wasn't about to get squeamish and blow his one chance. He also thought about going home tonight and telling Bryn he was already on the team. That would be sweet.

"No problem," he said, lowering his voice to what he hoped sounded like a tougher, meaner level. "If you need someone to keep things running smoothly on the ice, I'm your man." He stared back at Craig.

Craig's eyes narrowed. "I'm not talking little old

lady hits, Selkirk. I'm talking about all-out war. The Nighthawks take no prisoners."

Evan nodded. "That's the way I like to play." Then he added boastfully, "When I take a guy out, he stays out." This wasn't actually true. He'd never checked a guy in the hopes of hurting him so badly the player would be out of the game. Evan was sure the tough-talking captain of the Nighthawks was just testing him, nothing more.

There was a moment of awkward silence as though Craig was evaluating Evan in a new light.

"What number do you want on your jersey, Selkirk?" Craig said at last, slapping Evan on the back.

Evan blew out the breath he'd been holding unconsciously. He was in! He felt great. "I like 07 and if it's okay with the team, no name." He looked at Craig to see if he would object.

"Is that some kind of Indian superstition or something?" Craig asked. "You know, like it might bring *bad medicine* to the team if your name is on your jersey?"

Evan was surprised at this crazy idea, but decided it might be fun to have the Nighthawks think he was some kind of shaman for the team.

"Yeah, that's it. It would be unlucky to have my name on my jersey. Keep the name off and I guarantee we'll win." Years ago Evan had discovered a trick that helped him focus on the ice. If his name wasn't displayed on his jersey, opposing players didn't play verbal head games nearly as much as when they had a name to attach to a face. Somehow insulting number 07 wasn't as effective as bad-mouthing Evan Selkirk.

Craig nodded, agreeing. "Welcome to the Nighthawks, Selkirk."

"This is going to be a totally awesome season," Evan said more to himself than to Craig.

He felt elated as he changed into his street clothes. Things were going great. He was on the number one team in the league. The Nighthawks players were practically gods at school and now he was going to be in that elite group. All he had to do was live up to the tough guy image he'd given Craig Carpenter.

***

Their family meal was later than usual that night and both Evan and Bryn were eager with anticipation. Finally, after what seemed an eternity to the boys, the family sat down to dinner.

"You two look like a couple of cats who snacked on a canary. Out with it, what's happened." Julianne Selkirk smiled at her two boys, her chocolate-brown eyes shining.

Bryn and Evan looked at each other. Aware of the other's excitement and wanting to be first with the news, they both started talking at once. Neither stopped and both boys upped the volume to be heard.

"Whoa, too much noise! Bryn you're the oldest. You begin." Their dad pointed to Bryn with his fork. He winked at Evan, already knowing the good news his son had to share. Evan had told him on the ride home.

Bryn groaned at the old joke. He was the oldest. In fact, a day earlier than his brother. Okay, he'd been born ten minutes to midnight on January 16, and Evan had been born ten minutes after midnight, which technically made his birthday January 17. They always celebrated their birthdays on separate days, which threw people who knew they were twins, but the facts were the facts.

Bryn took a deep breath and told his story about how he came to be the newest member of the Comets hockey team, including all the details, except what he felt his parents didn't need to know, like the part about how much he liked Kelsey. His parents were especially impressed with how he had saved her from being run over by the speeding van.

Bryn also left out Kelsey's opinion of Indian people. He wanted his family to like her, in case they ever got the chance to actually meet.

"This is turning out to be quite the dinner for surprises," his dad said with a knowing grin.

"Since Kelsey's going to Westhaven, does she have a special musical talent also?" asked Bryn's mom, as she reached for a large bowl of mashed potatoes.

He thought about this for a moment. In view of her

opinion of musical bands and musicians, he seriously doubted Kelsey played any instrument.

"Ah, actually, we didn't talk much about music." He moved quickly to another topic. "Kelsey's dad teaches phys. ed. at Westhaven. Hey, did I mention Lucas is captain of the Comets and Mr. Coles is the head coach? I'm really looking forward to learning how to play hockey." He looked down at his plate. He'd never thought of playing before this had all started, but it was too late to back out now.

"It's odd the Comets are willing to take on a *raw rookie* who's never been in a game before this far into the season." Evan looked suspiciously over at Bryn, who avoided his gaze.

"Lucky break for me," Bryn said quickly as he shoved a huge forkful of salad into his mouth. Bits of lettuce hung out the corners of his lips and jerked up and down as he chewed.

"Brynley Selkirk, stop eating like a wild animal," his mother admonished.

Bryn grinned, exposing more of the leafy contents of his mouth. "Sorry, Mom," he mumbled, as a couple of pieces of carrot dropped out and back onto his plate.

His mom rolled her eyes.

"Mom, can I tell you my news now that Mr. Etiquette is done with the circus act?" Evan asked. Impatiently, he brushed his hair back out of his eyes.

Everyone's attention refocused on Evan.

"Absolutely." She folded her hands in her lap and waited.

"I'm going to be playing for the Nighthawks this season!" he announced proudly. "They're the number one team in the league and they're going to win the championship come Minor Hockey Week in January. I tried out this afternoon and Craig, the captain, says I'll start as a forward in this Saturday's game. I have a practice Friday night."

The boys' mother looked from one son to the other. "This is great! You gentlemen are amazing. Today is quite a triumph for the Selkirks and hockey. It's going to be a busy sports year."

"If both boys are on a team, the question is who won the bet?" Thomas asked.

"What if we up the ante?" their mother asked with a mischievous look. "Let's say that whoever's team finishes highest in the standings or actually wins the Minor Hockey Week championship takes the big prize." She thought a moment. "Wins what though?" She looked around the table. "A prize worthy of a champion. What about the admiration and good wishes of your entire family?"

"That's lame, Mom." Evan frowned. "I can decide on what my ultimate prize will be later." He said this with such confidence that his mother stopped and stared at him, one eyebrow raised.

"What?" Evan asked. "I told you the Nighthawks

were number one. They'll win all right. No doubt about it."

"Wrong again!" Bryn scoffed. "But you're right about one thing. I can decide what the prize will be after the championship goes to the best team in the league, *my team*!" He gave Evan a defiant stare, daring him to start something.

"We'll see then," their dad said. "And may the best team win!" He raised his glass of iced tea in a mock toast.

"I heard about the Nighthawks, Evan," Bryn began casually. "I talked to Lucas about other teams in the league, and the Nighthawks have a reputation for playing dirty and using a lot of force." He put his fork down and stared at his brother. "Consider this a friendly warning. Be careful. They play rough hockey and you might get hurt."

Evan's face went red. "Like you know what rough hockey is." He snorted at his brother. "I can take care of myself on the ice, Bryn. I won't be the one getting hurt." He rushed on, his voice sounding loud in the still room. "The Nighthawks are winners and I guess that makes me one too." He looked smugly at his brother before going back to his meal.

Bryn's eyes narrowed. "Yeah, I heard a lot of other stuff too, but I guess a smart guy like you can find out for yourself." His words of warning were left hanging in the air between them.

4 A JUGGLING ACT

Bryn felt strange as he carried his large hockey equipment bag down the hallway at school the next afternoon. He wasn't used to hauling the heavy bag and moved awkwardly with it. Rounding a corner, Bryn ran straight into Mr. Boothby.

"Oh man! I'm sorry. Are you okay?" Bryn asked as the old man steadied himself on his feet.

"Oh my, yes, Master Selkirk. I used to play rugby and never let a little scrum take me down." He noticed Bryn's equipment bag. "What's this? You're going to play hockey?"

He sounded surprised and Bryn wondered if it was because he somehow knew, using that mysterious instinct teachers have for detecting lying, that Bryn had never played before and was faking it.

"I'm on the Comets, sir. Kelsey and I are just heading over to the rink for my first practice," he explained proudly.

"Ah, yes, the lovely Miss Coles. She's been assigned

as your study buddy if I remember correctly." Mr. Boothby looked at Bryn for confirmation and Bryn nodded, grinning like an idiot. Then, to his never-ending embarrassment, his face became hot and his colour changed to scarlet.

Mr. Boothby didn't seem to notice his glowing cheeks.

"I believe her brother Lucas is involved also." The white-haired teacher's brow furrowed, creating even more ripples on his wrinkled face.

"He's the captain of the team, sir." Bryn informed the vice-principal helpfully.

"Ah, yes. Well, you'd better hurry along, young man." He nodded his head knowingly. "At your age, some things can't wait." He smiled kindly and headed off down the hall.

Bryn watched him go. He'd heard the other kids talk about this unusual teacher in terms which were not always kind. They called him the Headmaster, because of his English accent and strange mannerisms. Bryn disregarded their gossip. He liked the fussy old gentleman.

He spotted Kelsey waiting at the doors. "Hi, sorry I'm late." He hefted the heavy bag, adjusting it on his slim shoulders as they left the building. "I ran into Mr. Boothby."

Kelsey made a face. "He's such a weird teacher. Every time I do something wrong, I expect him to whip out a cane and give me a whack like in those old

British school movies." She giggled.

"He's not so bad. What does he teach here, anyway?" He was looking at Kelsey and the way the sun glinted off her auburn hair; he didn't notice the two steps down to the sidewalk.

The heavy equipment bag caused him to overbalance and his feet were suddenly treading air. He felt himself falling.

Kelsey rushed to help him up. "Bryn! Are you okay?"

"Watch that first step, it's a doozy," he said, blushing furiously and feeling like the world's biggest loser. Why did he always manage to look like an idiot when he was around Kelsey? He'd never been like this before meeting her.

As they walked, they began talking about the different things that interested them. Bryn liked the fact that Kelsey knew a lot of weird stuff and had read so many books. She had an incredible memory and could recall characters out of every book she'd read, including their names and what they did. She was smart and he found he could talk to her about almost anything. When the conversation turned to personal topics, though, Bryn steered Kelsey away from anything to do with music or people who were First Nations.

"Tell me about living up north," she asked. "Your dad is a teacher and your mom's a lawyer. Did you live in a house surrounded by Eskimos living in igloos?

Were you the only white people up there?"

Bryn knew most people who lived away from the north knew little about those who had thrived in Canada's arctic for thousands of years. "*Inuit* or *Innu,* not *Eskimo,*" he corrected gently. "To make it easy for you to remember, just think of it like this. People who live in the north on the west side of Hudson's Bay are *Inuit,* those who live on the east side are *Innu,* and they live in ordinary houses. There's lots of Cree people in Quebec and Labrador also."

"Inuit or *Innu,* got it," Kelsey nodded her head.

"Also," Bryn went on. "There were lots of other white people, but when it's blizzarding and the wind chill is minus seventy degrees, it doesn't matter who it is that pulls you out of the snowdrift when you're stuck." He pulled his coat around him and hefted his bag.

When they arrived at the rink, Bryn left her and went to change. He felt quite proud of the assortment of gear he had managed to come up with. True, everything was handed down from Evan, but Bryn didn't mind. It was all new to him. The night before, his dad had shown him how to dress in the layers of protective equipment that were required for league play. He'd practised dressing in his cumbersome getup until he could fasten all the buckles and straps in a reasonable time, making sure all the pieces were on the right way.

He laced his own old skates up and headed for the

ice. The Comets had a game next week and Bryn was hoping he could be ready by then. Kelsey would like that.

He moved out onto the icy surface and began warming up. Deliberately, he shut off the music he'd been playing quietly in the back of his brain. He had to concentrate.

His hockey stick felt big and awkward. Half the time, he wasn't sure what to do with the thing. He had wrapped tape around the place where Evan had written his name on the shaft.

Suddenly, Lucas skated in front of him and stopped with a shower of shaved ice.

"You must have different rules up in the frozen north."

Bryn looked confused. "Maybe, I'm not sure," he said truthfully. "Why?"

Lucas looked down at Bryn's old Bauer Junior Supreme skates. "Your skates. They haven't allowed those old style *tube skates* for a long time down here. I'm sure you must have newer ones for league play."

Bryn was confused. What were "tube skates" and why couldn't he use them? His were hardly worn at all, and he had always put thick brown polish on the leather to keep it shiny and put new laces in when the others became dirty. They may be old, but they didn't look it at all. Skates were skates up where he'd come from. It didn't matter if they were not this year's models. "Yeah, sure, I know they're old." He tried to sound casual. "These babies have a lot of rink time on them." He hoped this sounded like jock talk, but from the blank look on Lucas's face, he thought he'd better take a different approach.

"We haven't unpacked all our boxes from the move yet and I don't know where my new stuff is. I figured these old things would be okay for a practice." He thought that sounded like a good excuse.

"Sure, they'll be fine for practice." Lucas nodded agreeably. "You'll have to find your other pair or you won't be allowed on the ice. Those oldies are just too dangerous."

Bryn decided to ask his dad to take him to the mall and buy him new skates before his first game next week.

Lucas smiled and passed him the puck, which just managed to avoid hitting Bryn's stick. "You ready to rumble?"

Rumbling was a hockey term Bryn was not familiar with, but he was conscious of Kelsey watching. "You bet! I'm always up for a good rumble!" He hoped he could do it, whatever it was.

Lucas proceeded to take him through what he called *basic drills,* but which Bryn thought of as a gruelling, death-defying series of manoeuvres that no mere mortal could possibly do—especially on skates!

Lucas would pass and Bryn would miss. Lucas would deke and Bryn would miss. Lucas would shoot and Bryn would miss again. He couldn't seem to do anything right.

"You're a little off your game today. What's the matter?" Lucas asked as he effortlessly stripped the puck from Bryn's stick.

"It must be the change in altitude," Bryn said lamely. He was making an idiot of himself in front of Kelsey and could do nothing to stop the humiliation.

"I'm guessing you weren't on the first line of your old team," Lucas said, giving Bryn a light check which, since he was unprepared for it, sent him into the boards with a bone-jarring thump.

Lucas skated over and helped him up. "Sorry, Bryn. I didn't think I hit you that hard."

Bryn just shrugged and readjusted his helmet.

"Maybe that's enough for today," Lucas said, seeing the pained look on Bryn's face. "I'm about done myself."

"Sure, if that's what you think we should do," Bryn said, trying to keep from groaning. Every muscle in his body was screaming for mercy.

Kelsey waved from the bench and the two boys skated over.

"Bryn did great for his first time *at this altitude*," Lucas said with a shake of his head. "I think we should have one more practice before the game. Can you make it Sunday afternoon?"

"Sure, no problem." Bryn tried to smile, but even his face muscles ached.

"Hey, what do you say, want to go for burgers at the mall?" Kelsey asked. "Lucas is buying."

Bryn looked at his watch. It was nearly five o'clock. Five o'clock, hmmm...wasn't there something he was supposed to be doing? All of a sudden his stomach flipped in a tight circle and crashed into the boards. He had completely forgotten he was supposed to meet with his music instructor after school to evaluate his piano skills! He was in big trouble.

"I've got to go!" he said excitedly. "Ah, I'll take a rain check on that burger. I'm late for..." He didn't know what to say. He couldn't tell Kelsey he was supposed to be at piano class. She had just invited him on what was as close as he'd ever been to a date. "I'm late, I'm late for a really important date!" He winced as a vision of the white rabbit out of *Alice in Wonderland* hopped through his brain. "See you tomorrow," he called over his shoulder as, hurrying as fast as he could in the clumsy gear, he started for the dressing room. Kelsey was going to think he was an idiot, if she didn't already after that brilliant hockey demo he'd just blown. He didn't know why he'd played so extraordinarily badly this afternoon. What was different about today? Why hadn't he been able to click?

He put all thoughts of the blown hockey practice out of his mind as he started back to school. Maybe he could catch the piano teacher and apologize. Maybe he could still make it up. Dragging the heavy equipment bag on his shoulder, Bryn hurried back to Westhaven.

★★★

The school corridors were dark when Bryn reached the stately old school. He noticed the peculiar, but pleasant smell he associated with Westhaven. It was a mixture of well-used textbooks and old polished wood.

He made his way to the music room. "Be there, be there," he whispered to himself as he opened the worn oak door.

He'd never actually been to this room before. It was huge with tiered seats and had a stage large enough to accommodate an entire orchestra. The first thing Bryn saw upon walking in quietly was the piano. It was a beauty. A baby grand, gleaming black with glistening white keys.

Mesmerized, Bryn dropped his hockey bag and slowly walked toward the instrument. At home, they had an ancient second-hand upright that needed constant tuning. It was okay, but this...He ran his hand over the black satin surface, then, very tentatively, he reached out and pressed the middle C key.

The sound was clear and beautiful in the large room. The acoustics were awesome. Bryn's finger tingled where he touched the key. He felt a tightness in his chest like an ache. He desperately wanted to play the beautiful instrument.

"Why don't you sit and try it out, Master Selkirk?"

The voice was unmistakable. Bryn whirled around

to see Mr. Boothby standing in the doorway to the office marked Music Department Head. He swallowed. "Sir! I mean, Mr. Boothby, sir. Are you the piano teacher I was supposed to meet two hours ago for my evaluation?" He winced a little when he said it.

He waited for the blast to hit, but instead the old teacher just nodded his head. "I am. I told you some things *can't* wait. Fortunately for young men like you, some of us are willing to indulge these youthful flights of fancy." He waved casually in the direction of his office. "I also had a stack of papers to mark that kept me here, which is extremely fortunate for you."

Bryn didn't know what to say. He stood like a statue.

"Well, we're late enough already, Master Selkirk. Perhaps we'd better get started." Mr. Boothby indicated the piano with an impatient wave of his hand.

"Right, absolutely, sir." Bryn stumbled as he hurriedly sat himself at the piano. Slowly, with a careful touch, he reached out and placed his hands on the keyboard. Suddenly the music of Mozart filled his mind and his fingers began flying over the keys. He scarcely knew if he was in control of his own hands or they were somehow, magically, in control of him. He played on; the music soared and filled the huge, cavernous room.

At last, the dying notes trailed off into the corners of the room and Bryn sat back exhausted, but happy.

He had never played better. He knew he had done well.

Mr. Boothby cleared his throat, frowning slightly.

"Humph. Not as bad as I thought you'd be." He walked over and stood over Bryn. "Let's take it from the top and this time, I want you to put a little feeling into the piece. Remember, sometimes it's not the loudest notes that carry the most power. Begin..."

Bryn spent the next hour practising as he'd never done before. He soon came to realize how much he *didn't* know about music.

At last Mr. Boothby raised his hand. "That will do, Master Selkirk. I think we've tortured Mr. Mozart enough for one day. You may go." He dismissed Bryn without any comment on his playing.

"That's it, sir? That's all you have to say?" Bryn was floored. "But..." He didn't know how to ask about the Protégé Program. He must not have made the cut. He was so stupid. He'd gone to hockey practice and ticked off Mr. Boothby. Bryn sighed. "Good night, Mr. Boothby. And thank you once again for letting me play for you." He slowly trudged over to his equipment bag, and looking down at it, winced at the thought of lugging it home.

Bending over, Bryn pulled to lift up the heavy bag, then suddenly the sounds of his own playing flashed through his head. The beautiful notes echoed in his mind. He dropped the bag and turned to the old teacher. Excluding him from the program because he'd been late for one dumb appointment was unfair.

He could feel his temper rising. "You know, I never

believed the other kids when they said you were mean and weird. I thought you were kind of cool, in a strange English sort of way. But if you're nuking me from the Protégé Program just because I messed up and forgot a stupid appointment then maybe the other kids are right. I played well." He stopped and shook his head. "No, sir, I played better than that, I played *great* and I think it's really unfair of you to dump me because of one little scheduling mistake."

Bryn's heart was pounding and he was out of breath. He couldn't believe what he had said to a teacher who was not simply a teacher, but vice-principal and Music Department Head of the school he'd just transferred to this week! It made him feel a little dizzy.

Mr. Boothby's face was dark. "What in the name of Thor are you railing on about, young man?" Then he smiled. "After the first five minutes, there was never any question you would be admitted to the Protégé Program. The rest of our session, I was just enjoying the music. In fact, I think you should enter the Edmonton Piano Competition in January. Talent like yours should be showcased, and at a large competition such as that, you could really make a mark for yourself. It could be very important for your future."

Bryn was stunned. He couldn't think of anything to say.

"But keep in mind, your success depends on a lot of factors," Mr. Boothby went on. "Raw talent isn't enough to take you to the great concert halls, Master Selkirk. It's going to take dedication and hard work. You are going to have to practise, practise, practise." He crossed his arms against his chest. "And you won't always like the choices you're going to have to make."

Bryn couldn't believe it! He was going to be in the program after all and Mr. Boothby thought he had talent! "I'm in the Protégé Program?" he asked in a small voice. "And you think I'm good enough to enter a major competition?" Everything was happening so fast, he had to make sure it was real.

Mr. Boothby nodded his head.

"And don't worry about my practising, sir. I'll practise." Bryn couldn't stop smiling. "In fact, I love to practise. I'm going to go home and practise right now." He grabbed his bag as though it weighed no more than a page of sheet music. "Thank you, sir. Thank you."

★★★

By the time he reached home, the giddiness at being accepted into the Protégé Program was ebbing and Bryn thought he was going to die of exhaustion. The bus had been crowded and the other commuters had grumbled loudly at the space his bag took up. Every muscle, every bone, every molecule in his body wanted to leave to escape the pain.

"Mom, Dad! Wait till I tell you what happened

today!" He called as he dumped his equipment in the entryway and hobbled into the dining room. He sat down at the table across from Evan.

"Well, you have our full attention," his mom said handing him a plate of roast beef.

Bryn took a deep breath. "I played for Mr. Boothby today. He's the piano instructor at school..." He told the family all about his mini-recital and how he had gone nuts afterward only to find out Mr. Boothby had already decided to accept him into the program.

"I guess this means you're going to have to quit the Comets," Evan said leaning back in his chair, his hair straying down onto his forehead. "There's no way you can get your hockey skills up and play the piano too." He looked thoughtful. "Hey, isn't there something about keeping a B+ average to stay in your fancy piano program? I guess that means hitting the books pretty hard as well." Evan smiled in a smug way that made Bryn want to climb over the table and punch the look off his brother's face.

His words dripped malice, but everything he said was true. Bryn didn't care. There was no way he was going to let either his hockey or his piano go. "No, I think if I work hard, I can do it all," he answered with a confident smile.

Bryn tried to ignore his brothers comments, but later while trying to sleep, he thought about how busy his life was about to become. He remembered what

Evan had said about having to keep a B+ average and the extra hockey practices he'd need.

He hoped he hadn't taken on too much.

5 TEAM ORDERS

Evan discovered being the newest Nighthawk did make him a celebrity at school. He was at first surprised, then pleased when kids called him by name in the hallways. He had to remind himself to smile and return the friendly greetings. It wasn't natural for him, but he was determined to fit in.

There had been time for only one extra practice before his first game, but he was an experienced player and caught on quickly, and he now knew the team plays cold.

It was Saturday night and his first game as a Nighthawk was about to begin. They were playing the Inglewood Devils.

"You up to speed on all the plays, Selkirk?" Craig asked him as they did their warm-up skate.

"Like I wrote them," Evan answered confidently.

The game went well until the third period when the Devils put on a super effort and scored three goals in rapid succession, giving them a one-point lead.

"This just won't do," Craig said as he watched the two Devil forwards who had put on the scoring drive return to the ice. His voice was low and menacing. "I think it's time these guys learned what it means to go up against the Nighthawks." His eyes narrowed as he turned to Evan. "Here's where you get to show us why you're on the team, Selkirk. I want you to bust up their line. Take out those forwards and make sure they don't give us any more trouble. And Selkirk," he looked at Evan meaningfully, "don't worry if you take a penalty."

Evan nodded. He wasn't sure how much force Craig wanted him to use, but the message was clear. Take out the goal scorers from the Devils' hot front line.

He moved out to the faceoff circle and looked across at his first target. The guy was big and looked as if he could handle what was coming. Evan tightened his grip on his stick.

The puck dropped and everyone scrambled. Craig was the other Nighthawk forward. He out-muscled his man, took possession of the puck, then headed for the Devils goal. Trevor, playing centre, followed him across the blue line. Jamie and Tank stayed in defensive positions keeping themselves between the Devils line and the Nighthawks' goalie.

Totally focused, Evan zeroed in on his target. As soon as Craig started toward the net, Evan made his move. Using his stick, he reached out and caught the skate edge of the defenceman covering him. The ref missed that move entirely. The defenceman tripped and hit the ice.

Evan went after the Devils' forward who was moving to intercept the puck. Picking up speed, he came in fast, shoulder-checking the player hard into the boards. The beefy forward fell, grabbing his ankle as his leg twisted awkwardly beneath him.

Without a backward glance, Evan skated on. He caught up with the play in time to block the other Devils defenceman, which allowed Craig to do a slick wraparound and tie the score.

"Not bad, Selkirk," Craig said as they came off the ice. He handed Evan his water bottle. "Hurry up, you're going back out. You've got one more forward to squash."

When the next line change was called, Evan did as he was told. He hit the ice already searching out his target.

The guy was alone and Evan didn't think he looked like much of a threat this far behind the play, but orders were orders. He headed across the ice toward the unguarded skater.

Evan raised his stick, holding it in both hands across his body, and slammed into the guy. Just as he was hit, the young player looked up at his attacker, total surprise on his face. He hadn't expected the hit and was unprepared. He went down hard, his stick spinning away and one of his gloves flying off from the impact of Evan's cross-check. The whistle blew before the Devils forward had stopped sliding.

The ref's arms made the forward and backward motion in front of his chest signifying a cross-checking penalty. Evan didn't care. The other Devils forward was out.

Thanks to his taking out the two high-scoring forwards, the Nighthawks took back the lead and went on to win. Evan, enjoying the feeling of being one of the team, went with the guys for burgers after the game. He laughed and joked with Trevor, Jamie, and Craig as if he'd been on the team for years. Craig thought he was great, a real asset to the Nighthawks.

Evan tried not to think of the two players he'd blasted to make the win happen, but he couldn't get the surprised look of the young forward he'd cross-checked out of his mind. He shook it off. Sure, the Nighthawks had taken a lot of unnecessary roughing penalties, but this was hockey in the big leagues.

★★★

Evan knew his dad would want to talk to him when he came home. He could still hear the lectures on consideration for other players and fair play, which had become standard for his dad to dish out. After storing his hockey equipment, he went into the kitchen where his dad was waiting.

"There you are, son," his dad said, without his usual smile. "That was quite the game for your first as a Nighthawk."

Evan hesitated. "Ah, yeah, Dad. We won and that's what's important. You know, we're not that far away from Minor Hockey Week and we want to be the team to beat."

His dad looked him straight in the eyes. "If you keep using the same tactics you did today, I sure wouldn't want to be up against you. I thought you played a little rough."

Evan felt his pulse go up. "Dad, that's the way hockey is played down here. This isn't some bush league team from Whapmagoostui or Labrador." He grabbed a can of pop out of the fridge and went to his bedroom. He'd had enough after-game discussion.

As he walked past Bryn's room, he heard the crashing sounds of a wild symphony booming from behind the closed door.

"Turn that screaming noise down!" he yelled, hammering his fist on his brother's door as he walked past.

Bryn opened the door. "That happens to be Beethoven's Fifth Screaming Noise and I won't turn it down." He closed the empty CD case he'd been holding. "I saw you play today. I told you that team had a reputation for vicious hockey. I just didn't realize my brother would be their number-one goon. Is that what it took to get on the team, Evan? You have to be the enforcer?" He raised his eyebrows questioningly.

Evan shot him a dirty look but his face was burning. "And what did it take for you to get on the Comets? What did you have to put up with to get on that team? At least I can live up to my press. I can play hockey that will make your head spin."

"More like take my head off, if today was any indication!" Bryn snapped, then turned and slammed the door.

Evan ignored his parting shot and went to his room. Bryn just didn't understand what it took to play in the big leagues.

6 BROTHER VS. BROTHER

Bryn's practice went very well on Sunday, and he discovered that with his new Bauer skates, he had more power and could skate faster. He was amazed at the difference good equipment could make. He and his dad had bought his skates the previous day and when Bryn had tried them on, he had felt like the newest draft choice in the NHL.

"Hey, have you been practising at home?" Lucas asked as Bryn smoked past and slammed the puck into an empty net.

Bryn shook his head, turning off the music that had been accompanying him as he rushed the net. "New skates!" he laughed. "I feel like I could take on the Edmonton Eskimos and skate them into the ice!"

Lucas looked at him quizzically. "The Eskimos? Yeah, you could probably out-skate some of them—especially the fullbacks. You must have been really out of touch when you lived up north. The Eskimos are a football team. I think you mean the Oilers. You know—Wayne Gretzky, five Stanley Cups..."

Bryn cursed himself. He was an idiot. He should shut up and not try and do the jock-talk thing. It just wasn't his style. Concentrating on following exactly what Lucas said, Bryn started to catch on and actually enjoyed the rest of the practice. Lucas gave him lots of great coaching advice. If the goalie is deep, shoot at the corners. High shots are usually caught and held, while low shots create rebounds, so shoot low. He had adjusted the length of his stick also and now it felt as if he had a useful tool instead of a meter-and-a-half-long snowplow. By the time they finished practice, Bryn was feeling better about his ability to help the Comets.

Lucas looked at him quizzically. "Do you think you're ready for Thursday night?" he asked.

"Thursday night?" Bryn said, instantly panicked. His scheduled audition for the Edmonton Piano Competition was Thursday night. Mr. Boothby had said it was important to his future. How had Lucas found out about it? "Thursday night?" he repeated, wondering how much Lucas knew. "Who told you? Does your sister know?" He looked over at Kelsey who was waiting in the penalty box. She smiled and waved.

Lucas stopped in mid-stride as they were coming off the ice. He looked at Bryn and frowned. "What do you mean, who told me? My dad, the *coach* told me, and besides, the schedule's posted. We're playing Thursday night at the Cross Arena. Kelsey knows, but why does it matter if she does or not?"

Bryn knew he had messed up again. This secret identity stuff was hard. "Hockey? Sure, I meant the hockey game Thursday." Then he realized what Lucas had asked. "Do I think I'm ready for a game?" he repeated excitedly. "You bet! This is so cool! What position will I play?" Calming himself, he waited for Lucas to continue speaking.

"I think you'll work best on defence." Lucas smiled at Bryn. "Did you get this enthusiastic when you played up north?"

"Oh, it's just this is my first game..." Bryn realized what he'd said. "I mean, down here...with a big-city team like the Comets." He groaned inwardly. Yeah, he'd really covered that one smoothly, but Lucas didn't seem to notice this blunder.

Just then, Kelsey joined them. "I told you he'd be ready for Thursday's game!" She punched her brother on the arm, then turned to Bryn. "Bryn, you played great! I'm proud of you." Her smile warmed Bryn right down to his skate blades.

"I just hope I don't let the team down," he said, embarrassed—but he meant it. All he had to do was bail out of the biggest piano recital he'd ever had!

***

That night Bryn lay awake worrying how he could be

in two places at once. Maybe he should just stop trying to hide his music from Kelsey, he thought, but they were getting along *so* well. In fact, she'd invited him over to watch a movie. There had to be a way, all he had to do was think of it.

Then it hit him. "That's it!" he said, sitting up in bed. A movie! He'd *record* his performance with a video camera, then burn it onto a DVD and plead with Mr. Boothby to ask the committee to allow it in. The committee would decide if he was good enough to enter the Edmonton competition. The video was a way to let him be in two places at once without anyone being the wiser. Old Boothby would do it—especially if Bryn told him this was the one and only time he would do this.

By Wednesday, he was ready. He'd chosen a Beethoven sonata, a favourite, which was a little above the level he was comfortable playing, but if he could pull it off, it would sound spectacular. He waited till after school, then went to Mr. Boothby's office with his family's new digital video camera.

"Excuse me, sir," he said quietly, interrupting the old teacher.

"Ah, if it isn't Master Selkirk. Shouldn't you be practising for tomorrow night?" he asked, looking at Bryn over the top of tiny, half-rimmed spectacles.

"That's actually why I'm here, Mr. Boothby." Bryn took a deep breath and explained his plan. Mr. Boothby sat and listened quietly until Bryn had finished.

"I told you that there would be difficult choices for you to make, and that you would have to choose piano over everything else to succeed." Sighing as he took off his glasses, Mr. Boothby sat rubbing his eyes and thought for a moment.

Bryn's heart sank. If Mr. Boothby didn't go along with this, he wasn't sure what he'd do.

"Knowing how important the Comets are to you," the old teacher began, then replacing his glasses, he looked at Bryn over the tops of them. "Or at least some of the people associated with the Comets, I think under the circumstances we could try your ingenious solution." The old teacher stood up. "I have just the thing." He left the office, then came back several moments later. "Well, don't just sit there, come along, come along." He took the camcorder from Bryn. "Go get warmed up while I set this contraption on this tripod."

Bryn scrambled to the piano and took out his sheet music. When he was ready, he nodded at Mr. Boothby who switched on the camera.

Bryn began to play and he played fabulously. He not only saw the notes on the page, but all around him they soared and floated freely in space. His head was filled with the perfect music. His fingers felt as though an unknown force possessed them. He forgot about time or where he was. There was only the music.

Finally, he played the closing notes. The room echoed

with the sudden stillness the silence brought with it. Mr. Boothby looked first at him, then at the camera.

"Shall we see how this little machine did?" he asked. Bryn nodded, extremely pleased with his performance. He had never played like that before.

They rewound the tape and hit the play button. A small tinny noise issued from the box. Bryn looked fine in the minuscule screen, but the music, his beautiful music, sounded terrible. "I guess this machine's not made for a special job like this," he said, sagging with disappointment. "I can't submit that for my performance. It stinks." He hoped his voice sounded steady.

"I agree." Mr. Boothby said shaking his head. "That's why I took the liberty of also using the machine the school has for just such a purpose." He walked over to a large cabinet and reaching inside, played with some dials and switches. "Let's have a look at how this one turned out." A huge screen dropped from the ceiling against the wall at the back of the stage.

The lights dimmed in the room and suddenly there on the big screen was Bryn, sitting at the baby grand. And then the music started. Bryn was not prepared for the sound. He had heard his music before, but never like this. Every note, every nuance of the music was preserved. Bryn couldn't believe he was the one making that beautiful noise.

When it was over, Mr. Boothby just nodded. "That will do nicely for your entry. There is one thing I want to impress on you, Master Selkirk." He turned hard, flint-grey eyes on Bryn. "Music, especially when it concerns someone of your potential, is not to be taken lightly. This is the last time we will do anything like this. In the future, I expect you to live up to your obligations."

"I will sir, I promise. Thanks, Mr. Boothby." Bryn left, fully intending to live up to his promise.

★★★

The night of the game, Bryn and his parents arrived early at the Cross Arena. Bryn was so excited he could hardly sit still. Evan also had a game, but he was going with Craig Carpenter and a couple of other Nighthawks players.

Bryn felt great. He took longer than usual to suit up because he wanted everything just right. Stepping out on the ice, he began his warm-up skate. He felt like a real hockey player in his dark blue uniform with the stylized star streaking across his chest. Kelsey was sitting in the stands behind the Comets' bench and gave him the thumbs up when he skated past.

"You okay with this?" Lucas asked as he caught up with Bryn.

"Sure. This is going to be great." Bryn tried to sound confident.

"It's just that the Nighthawks are a deadly team to face off against in your first game." Lucas nodded at the swarm of black uniformed players that had just come onto the ice.

Bryn nearly tripped over his new skates. The Nighthawks! He moved to the boards and began scanning the circling players. Suddenly there was Evan. He looked so much bigger in his uniform.

"Don't worry. You're going to be great!" Kelsey's voice from behind the Plexiglas at rinkside made Bryn turn. He smiled at her through his protective facemask.

She placed the palm of her hand against the glass. "Good luck, Bryn."

He nodded and turned back to the circling Nighthawks players. One player had stopped and was watching him. Bryn knew without even looking that it was Evan.

7 THE GIRL AT THE GLASS

The game was fast, just the way Evan liked it. He had hardly believed his eyes when he'd seen Bryn talking to that girl. It was obvious why his brother was suddenly interested in hockey. He'd seen a notice on Bryn's desk at home saying there was a piano recital tonight and he was sure his brother would opt for the piano. Evan knew music was Bryn's life. So why was he here? The answer had to be the girl at the glass.

Without consciously thinking about it, Evan checked a Comets player into the boards and kept skating. His brother must have temporarily lost his mind. He should be at the piano recital, not here, playing five minutes out of every period because he was so lame.

Evan came off the ice on a shift change and noticed Craig and Trevor talking and watching one of the Comets' players.

"How'd you like a little fun, Selkirk?" Craig asked.

"Sure, what's up?" Evan asked.

"See that geek on the Comets? We want you to

go out there and grind him into the ice. Lucas Coles needs a lesson and word has it this guy is his little buddy." Craig nodded toward the ice and when Evan saw which player he meant, he swallowed hard. It was Bryn.

Evan had heard some other Nighthawks talking about how Craig hated Lucas Coles. For the past two seasons, Lucas had out-gunned and out-skated Craig whenever they played against each other, and Craig wanted revenge. The idea of using Bryn to get at Lucas didn't sit well with Evan.

"That loser's no threat. He can hardly work the puck down the ice, let alone score." Evan said, trying to deflect the Nighthawks captain, but the look on Craig's face made it clear.

"I think smashing Coles's newest player *is* what we're after. What's the matter with you, Selkirk? You signed on as our muscle, and so far, you're doing a great job; but don't get me wrong, you can be replaced." His eyes narrowed ominously. "I want the message clear. We took him out just because we could and we can take any other player out, too. Nighthawks rule! Now, are you one of us or not?"

"Don't worry about me, Craig," Evan said through gritted teeth. "Like you said, Nighthawks rule." He was not going to let his jerk brother spoil the best thing he'd ever been in.

Evan hit the ice, moving rapidly toward Bryn. He'd have to take him out, but the idea of smashing his defenceless brother made him feel sick. Bryn was no threat to the Nighthawks' scoring. There must be a way around this.

Up ahead, Evan could see Bryn trying to keep up to the action. His helmet was bobbing and Evan knew his brother had his head tunes going. Bryn was skating better than Evan had ever seen him. He was handling his stick well also, smooth and coordinated. When had Bryn turned into a hockey player? If this was what having a girlfriend did for his nerdy brother, then he should always have one.

There was a sudden scuffle near the Comets net as two players diced over the puck. Jamie Carver came out of nowhere and crashed into the two, sending the puck spinning wildly out of control.

Evan watched as the puck headed straight for Bryn, who was standing absolutely still on the ice, waiting. Evan noticed his brothers helmet had also stopped moving. With a sudden awkwardness that was hard to look at, Bryn gathered the puck onto his stick and turned toward Paco Jenkins and the Nighthawks' goal.

Unbelievable! Bryn had a breakaway. A fan was waving a pennant and yelling so loudly, it caught Evan's attention. It was the dark-haired girl from the glass and she was cheering her hero on. He watched as Bryn tried to wave back with one gloved hand while herding the puck toward the goal with his stick.

Evan sped up, an idea coming to him. He skated up

beside his brother. "I have to take the puck, Bryn! Get out of the way!" he shouted.

Bryn looked at him like he was crazy. "Get lost, Evan!"

"Give me the puck or I'll cream you!" Evan yelled. "I'll have to, Bryn."

Bryn shook his head defiantly and moved jerkily on toward the goal.

Evan had no choice and it was going to be ugly. Just as he set himself to check Bryn hard into the boards, he saw how his brother was handling the puck. He was making a rookie mistake and tapping the puck too far forward of his stick, then catching up and tapping it again. This left the puck unprotected long enough for someone of Evan's ability to take advantage. Evan timed his strike, then reached out with his long stick and scooped the puck away from Bryn. It was as easy as taking candy from a baby. The crowd laughed and cheered the slick stickhandling.

Evan spun around and tore down to the Comets' net. With a quick deke which had the goalie moving sideways in the crease, Evan fired a backhand shot at the open lower corner. Clean goal!

As he skated toward the Nighthawks' bench, Evan couldn't help but notice the glare his brother gave him.

"I told you to take that guy out!" Craig growled as Evan sat down.

"I thought a goal would be even better. You know,

show the Comets we dominate the ice." Evan knew Craig had wanted a show of how tough the Nighthawks were, but they'd have to do it another way.

"Next time, it goes down just the way I say. That's why I wear the big C, got it?" Craig said jerking a thumb at the captain's insignia on his uniform.

Evan just nodded and looked away

★★★

Bryn was angry as he changed out of his uniform. He kept going over the missed chance at his first goal. He had tried so hard. He'd even shut the music off in his head so he could concentrate better on his technique.

Bryn couldn't believe how his brother had humiliated him in front of everyone, in front of Kelsey. He'd felt like an idiot having the puck so easily stripped from him on his very first breakaway. He'd been on his way to a goal! Instead of cheers all he could remember was the crowd laughing.

The more he thought about it, the angrier he became. Grabbing his equipment bag, he stormed into the Nighthawks changing room. Evan was the only player left.

"Why'd you do it?" Bryn demanded. Evan stopped what he was doing and stared at his brother. "You just couldn't stand the idea of me actually showing you up at your own game, could you?" Bryn was so angry; he could feel the heat rippling through his entire body.

Evan looked surprised. "Look, Bryn, all I did is take advantage of a rookie who couldn't protect the puck. Believe me, you came off lucky. There are a lot worse things that could have happened to you." He zipped his large equipment bag shut with a jerk. "You're just mad because your *girlfriend* was watching and I helped her see what a loser you really are."

At the mention of Kelsey, Bryn's anger spilled over into fury. "Leave her out of this. She had nothing to do with it!" But even as he said the words, he knew Evan had touched a nerve. He *had* wanted to score in front of Kelsey.

Evan reached for his stick. "The rest of the team is waiting for me. We're going out to celebrate our win over the Comets." He stopped and looked at Bryn suspiciously. "Hey, I thought you were supposed to be at some fancy piano thing tonight? What are you doing here playing second-rate hockey? If you wanted to impress your girl so much, you should have taken her to the recital. If she's heard you play, she knows you do better with a keyboard than a hockey stick."

Bryn felt a guilty look come over his face.

Evan stopped, studying his brother. "She does know about your piano, doesn't she?" he asked.

Bryn didn't know what to say. Despite all the practise he'd had lately, lying didn't come very naturally to him, especially with his brother who knew him so well.

"Don't worry about the recital," he said, dismissing the question. "I took care of that. Kelsey thinks my musical ability is...really great!" he added weakly, but knew it was too feeble to fool his brother.

"She doesn't know, does she?" Evan started to grin, his dark eyes flashing. "What's the matter? Does she think piano players are wimpy losers, so you decided to impress her with your hockey talent instead?"

Bryn couldn't believe how his brother had figured it all out so easily. "Forget it!" he yelled.

Evan shook his head and sighed. "Look, Bryn, I'm sorry for the crack about you playing second-rate hockey and the other stuff. In fact, I was going to tell you how impressed I was. Those extra lessons have paid off, because you looked good out there tonight." He shrugged. "I had no idea you could skate that well and despite what happened, you handled the lumber pretty slick."

Bryn was surprised. Evan handing out compliments was unheard of. "I...ah, well...thanks, Evan," he mumbled.

Just then Craig Carpenter walked into the dressing room. "What's the hold up, Selkirk? This guy causing you any trouble." His voice was menacing.

Evan turned away and quickly grabbed his bag with a vicious jerk. Bryn noticed his sudden change in attitude.

"Nothing I can't handle," Evan said, pushing roughly

past Bryn. "This loser Comet had some comment about how I stripped him of his only scoring chance for the whole season."

Craig started to laugh. "*Only scoring chance,* good one, Selkirk. From what I saw, you could be right." Laughing, Evan and Craig left the dressing room.

Bryn watched his brother walk away.

8 EVAN'S SECRET

Bryn didn't speak to Evan for days after the game.

Evan didn't care. He was busy with his new buddies, and the fame of being a hero at school was great. He'd started staying out with his friends more than his parents liked but they were hicks from the north and didn't realize what life in the big city was like.

He was having a few problems at school. Evan had to admit his grades were slipping a little. There had also been a couple of fighting incidents, which had earned him another lecture from his parents. Evan still fumed when he thought of those losers. They'd deserved what they got. His only regret had been his parents finding out.

Late on the following Saturday afternoon, Craig, Trevor and Jamie were hanging out at the food court at the mall. The other boys were busy throwing french fries around while Evan tried to finish his burger.

"This is lame," Craig said when he'd run out of ammo. "I've got some shopping to do. You got any money, Selkirk?"

Evan didn't have much on him, but he did have his bank card. "Come on. I can get some cash." He dropped the remnants of his burger on the table, grabbed his coat and headed for an ATM.

"How much do you want to borrow?" he asked casually as he shoved the card into the slot.

Craig raised an eyebrow. "*Borrow*? How much you got?"

Evan took out a hundred dollars from his savings, flashing the crisp twenties as he pocketed his card.

"Great, Selkirk! I guess you're buying!" Craig slapped him on the back and together the four headed for the department store at the far end of the mall. Evan felt great.

At the store, they bought a lot of junk with his money; candy, magazines, and Craig wanted a T-shirt but couldn't make up his mind whether to get one with the San Jose Sharks or the Boston Bruins logo on it.

"I need a couple of cans of this spray paint for some work at home," Jamie said as he held up two large cans of fluorescent purple and green paint.

Evan shrugged. "Whatever, put it in the basket." He paid for the purchases, then they all left the store. Jamie and Trevor were giggling and elbowing each other.

They had walked only a couple of steps, when a large man with grey hair stepped in front of them. "You four will have to accompany me back into the store."

Evan was confused. The man took a step toward

Trevor. Suddenly, Trevor pulled a T-shirt out from under his jacket and threw it at the man's face.

"Run!" he yelled, bolting past the man who was busy batting at the shirt and cursing.

Evan stood shocked, staring at the store detective. The man's face was very red as he reached a large beefy hand toward Evan.

"Come on," Craig yelled as he grabbed Evan's arm.

Evan started running too. They ran across the street and into an alley, which led to a field a couple of blocks away. By the time they reached the empty field, the other boys were laughing and punching one another.

"Did you see that guy's face? I thought he was going to explode!" Jamie laughed.

"Man, that was great, really great!" Trevor said excitedly, his eyes shining. He extracted another T-shirt from under his coat, displaying it like a trophy. It had a Boston Bruins logo on it. "Mission accomplished," he laughed and tossed the shirt to Craig.

"Whew!" Craig blew out a lungful of air. "I saw you boost the shirts, but I had no idea that rent-a-cop was going to bust you. Trev, you're losing your touch." He shook his head.

Evan was speechless. He didn't know what to say. He had never stolen anything in his life before and it scared him, but these guys were laughing like it was some kind of big joke. He tried to be cool about it. "You guys could have warned me, that shop-cop just about had me."

"Next time, I'll give you the heads up," Craig offered, punching him on the arm. "You'd better take that stuff home with you, Selkirk. If my mom finds any more loot I can't produce a receipt for, she threatened to toss me out on my ear."

"Sure," Evan agreed, but his stomach was twisted in knots.

★★★

Three days later, the Nighthawks had another hockey game. Craig got a hat trick and Evan had two goals and three assists. They won, but by the end of the game, the team had taken so many penalties the officials wanted to talk to the coach.

"Can you bring the T-shirt and spray paint to school tomorrow?" Craig asked Evan when they were changing after the game.

"Sure." Evan pulled his sweater over his head. He still felt bad about the shoplifting incident.

Craig, Trevor, and Jamie met Evan in the parking lot of the school the next morning.

"Did you bring the stuff?" Craig asked before Evan could say hello.

"Yeah, it's in my backpack," Evan said frowning.

He started to unzip the pack but Craig reached out a hand and stopped him.

"Not here. Come on, let's go over to the park." The

boys started across the street, laughing and talking; soon Evan felt more relaxed again. So Trevor had taken one lousy T-shirt. Did the rent-a-cop have to come after them like it was a federal case? The store had the other shirt back didn't they? Evan decided it wasn't really that important after all. He wasn't going to let it spoil his friendship with his new buddies.

"It's a great day, don't you think, Jamie?" Craig said grinning slyly.

"You know, I do believe you're right, Craig." Jamie smiled back knowingly at Craig.

"Perhaps we shouldn't let a nice day like this one go to waste by sitting in a stinking classroom. Who votes for a school holiday for all Nighthawks?" Jamie and Trevor immediately stuck up their hands. "What about you, Selkirk? You in or should I say *you out*?" Craig asked, laughing at his own joke.

Evan smiled weakly. He'd stayed up late last night studying for a test today and was sure he would get a great mark, but skipping school was something else he'd never done. It might be fun. "Sure, I'm *out*," he said, nodding at Craig.

They spent the day at the arcade and eating at three different fast food joints. Evan was having a great time. They wandered all over the neighbourhood and Craig pointed out places where he and the other boys had done things some might consider a little illegal.

"Dude, will you look at this place? Old Fogiesville

or what?" Jamie said as they sat stuffing themselves with candy bars bought with the last of another hundred dollars Evan had donated. They were sitting in a park with a large war memorial dedicated to all the soldiers who had died fighting for Canada.

"It could use a little sprucing up, wouldn't you say?" Craig suggested. "Where's that spray paint you brought, Selkirk?"

Evan suddenly became nervous. "Why do you want the paint?" he asked.

"Why do you think?" Craig said reaching for Evan's backpack. Evan grabbed for it, but was too late. Craig found the cans of paint, handed one to Jamie, and kept one for himself. "Let's add some artwork to that old chunk of concrete." He indicated the memorial.

Glancing around to make sure the park was empty, Evan watched as the other boys sprayed weird designs and patterns onto the statue.

"Your turn, Selkirk," Craig said, handing Evan the fluorescent purple spray paint.

"Ah, no, I don't think..." Evan began. Watching someone else do the graffiti was one thing, but actually doing it himself, that was quite another.

"What's the matter, Selkirk, you chicken?" Craig asked, his voice suddenly hard.

Brushing his hair off his forehead, Evan reluctantly took the paint. "Okay, it's just that I don't know what to write." He held the can awkwardly.

"Just don't sign your work,"Trevor laughed, a braying sort of sound, which was really irritating.

Evan didn't know what to draw, so he quickly sketched a crude figure, rather small and in an inconspicuous place, but he did it. He felt bad about defacing the old memorial, but the other boys seemed to think it was cool.

Later, as Evan was walking home, he thought of everything new he'd done these past few weeks. He'd liked the feeling of importance taking all that money out of the bank. In fact, when the guys had wanted burgers after the graffiti episode in the park, Evan had told them no problem and they simply stopped at another bank machine.

He remembered how his pulse had pounded when they had run from the store cop and how the guys thought he was cool after he'd spray-painted with them. It was like some kind of initiation into the Nighthawks. He was part of their group now. He was on the inside, for once.

Evan walked into the house and heard Bryn practising the piano. It was a sound as familiar to him as his own breathing. The music stopped and Bryn came into the kitchen where Evan was busy making a peanut butter sandwich.

"Where have you been?" Bryn asked, frowning.

"Nowhere, why?" Evan said, trying to sound casual.

"Because your *school* called and said you and three

other boys had skipped. The three guys are known for taking unscheduled holidays from class and you were seen with them." Bryn shook his head. "How could you be so dumb? Did you think the school wouldn't notice if half the Nighthawks went missing for a day?"

Evan felt a little dizzy. "Where are Mom and Dad now?"

Bryn folded his arms across his chest. "When the school secretary called and asked where you were, no one knew. That's when the principal asked them to come to the office for a little talk."

Carefully replacing the jar of peanut butter in the cupboard, Evan went up to his room. He no longer wanted the sandwich; he felt sick to his stomach.

9 THE SECRET SYMBOL

"What's the matter, Bryn? You look like you've lost your best friend." Kelsey nudged him with her elbow as they walked down the crowded hallway.

He'd been thinking about his brother and what had happened earlier this week when Evan skipped school. When his parents had come home, skipping wasn't the only thing they talked to Evan about. A security guard at the mall had recognized the boy caught shoplifting and called the school. The boy, Trevor Wells, was one of four boys who had been involved in the incident. There had been a lot of loud talk between his parents and Evan about responsibility and rules and breaking the law. Evan had become angry, saying he hadn't stolen anything. After everything had settled out, Evan was grounded.

Bryn felt bad for his brother, but it was his own fault for being so stupid. He hadn't even had a chance to tell Evan his good news. He'd been accepted to compete in the big piano competition in Edmonton! Mr. Boothby had told him yesterday and they were already deciding on which piece he would play. He felt a little giddy just thinking about it.

Bryn looked over at Kelsey. It was the most exciting thing that had ever happened to him, and he hadn't told Evan and couldn't tell Kelsey.

"...And we can always use more volunteers. What do you say? Do you want to come with me?" Kelsey looked at him for an answer, but he hadn't heard a word she'd said.

"Sure, count me in." He smiled at her. "Who, why, what, when, where?" he asked, hoping she'd explain things again.

Kelsey giggled. "After school, by the doors. Weren't you listening?" she asked, her clear brown eyes shining.

Bryn pretended to look hurt. "Hey, I got every word. Don't worry, I'll be there." She waved goodbye and as he watched her walk away, he wondered what he'd volunteered for.

★★★

When Bryn saw Kelsey after school, he felt a little apprehensive.

"Ready?" she asked, as they headed out to a waiting bus.

"You bet," Bryn said, nodding enthusiastically. "Where exactly are we going?"

"Over to the Veterans Memorial Park. There was some vandalism there and we're on cleanup detail." Kelsey sat and Bryn plunked himself next to her. "It's a good thing the chinook blew in last night and warmed the temperature up so we can paint."

Suddenly it all became clear to Bryn. "This has to do with you being on the student council again, right?"

Kelsey sighed, exasperated. "I told you the council has a Good Deeds Committee, which scouts out things we as concerned teenagers can do for our community." She said this part as if reading from a pledge card. "Today, we're going to paint over the graffiti some idiots sprayed on the statue in the park."

They arrived at the park and all the kids piled out of the bus with brooms, brushes, and paint.

"Wow, whoever did this made a real mess," Kelsey said, looking at the garish paint sprayed everywhere.

Everyone set to work cleaning the statue of old pigeon droppings, dead leaves, and the awful graffiti. Then Kelsey handed Bryn a paintbrush and a can of paint that was the same colour as the concrete.

"Pick your spot and start covering the mess up," she said grabbing another can for herself. "I wish we could catch whoever did this. I'd make sure the local paper ran their pictures and told the world who these idiots are."

As Bryn started painting, he began reading some of the slogans and names hoping one of the vandals had slipped up and left a clue as to who they were. He was just finishing painting over one particularly nasty phrase, in which two of the words were spelled wrong, when his brush stopped in mid-swipe. He stared at a strange figure painted on the concrete.

"I know, none of us knew what that one was either," Kelsey said. "It looks kind of like a man with his arms out, but why it's in pieces stacked on top of one another, we couldn't figure out." She scrunched up her delicate eyebrows. "There's something familiar about it though..."

Bryn dipped his brush in the grey paint and ran a thick brushstroke across the figure. "It probably doesn't mean anything," he said as he quickly painted out the remaining parts of the picture. He knew what the figure was. It was a symbol so familiar he'd known it from childhood. It was a stylized *inukshuk*, and the only person who drew one like that was Evan.

This was the final straw. His brother had done some really dumb things lately, but this was the limit. He was out of control. If the police found out about this on top of the shoplifting and skipping school, Evan would end up in juvenile court and he could say goodbye to ever becoming a lawyer. Bryn had no choice. He would have to talk to his brother.

10 FUTURE CONSIDERATIONS

"Are you nuts?" Bryn asked as he burst into Evan's room later that same evening.

Evan looked up at him from his stamp album where he was carefully arranging his latest acquisitions.

"If anyone had seen that *inukshuk* you painted on the memorial, they would have asked who had any association with the Innu and *bingo,* you'd be here in handcuffs. How would it look for a future lawyer to be arrested for defacing public property?" Bryn was furious.

Evan carefully finished replacing the stamp he'd been inspecting into his album. "Anyone could have painted an *inukshuk*. There's a picture of one on a forty-seven-cent Canadian stamp, for crying out loud. Besides, how would they trace it to a student from Turner?" he said smugly.

It was no good trying to talk to his brother.

Frustrated, Bryn turned to leave when suddenly he noticed a stack of familiar-looking slips tossed casually on Evan's dresser. "Holy smokes, what are these?" he asked, grabbing a handful of the papers.

Evan reached out and snatched the ATM withdrawal receipts back. "None of your business. I've got some work to do. So why don't you take a hike."

"Evan, that money is for when you go to university. You're not supposed to be touching it." Bryn was practically shouting now.

Evan's face went beet red. "Get out!" he shouted, shoving Bryn out of the room. "And mind your own business!" The door slammed in Bryn's face.

★★★

Later that week, Bryn was in Mr. Boothby's office discussing whether to play a piece by Bach called Three Part Invention (Sinfonia) in D-major or—and this was Bryn's favourite—Nine Variations in A-major by Ludwig van Beethoven.

"The Beethoven is too difficult. Perhaps you need something less taxing for your first competition," Mr. Boothby said, pursing his lips.

"I have a feeling for Ludwig van B.," Bryn began. "His music sort of speaks to me. I really think that's the piece for me." He could already hear the beautiful music in his head.

Sighing, Mr. Boothby relented. "Have it your way. I'll arrange for you to have access to the baby grand after school. You will be able to practise regularly on a fine instrument and still be home in time to do your school assignments. You can begin tonight." His face broke into a thousand crinkled lines as he smiled at Bryn. "I think that with hard work, you, Master Selkirk, are going to—what's the Canadian expression?—*bring the house down.*"

Bryn couldn't believe it! "No worries. I've always loved practising. Nothing could keep me away." He felt so great, he wasn't sure if it was legal!

He continued feeling great right up until he bumped into Kelsey on her way to class. "Just the guy I'm looking for," she said tossing her thick, curly hair back over her shoulder.

"What can I do for you, Miss Coles?" Bryn asked, mimicking Mr. Boothby's clipped British accent.

Kelsey smiled winningly. "You still haven't seen my new DVD of the best band of all time, Ragged Edge. I'm inviting you to come over to my house to watch, then have a bite of supper before heading over to the rink for the game tonight." She moved a little closer. "Since your house is not far from the rink, we could swing by and pick up your equipment. What do you say? Shall I pencil you in?" She waited expectantly.

The game had slipped his mind, but he could easily fit it in after piano practice. Several other things whirled through Bryn's head at once. First, how was he going to get out of going to Kelsey's house without hurting her feelings? He was committed to his piano practice.

And second, why did these things always happen to him? This would be twice he'd turned Kelsey down. Maybe there would never be a third chance to accept. Then there was the part about "swinging by his place." What if his mom was home? How would he explain this Cree woman living at his house or, for that matter, his brother Evan who looked so much like their mom?

He had to come up with an excuse. "I can't," he began, stumbling over his words. "Because..." He had to think of something fast. "I..." He was losing the battle. He noticed an old hamburger wrapper in the trash basket next to the lockers. Suddenly, Bryn had a brainstorm. It would solve a big problem for him. "I have a new part time job at the Burger Barn. I'll be tied up every night after school." He saw her disappointed look, but knew Kelsey was a strict vegetarian and would never be caught dead in a place that served pig parts or cow carcass.

She screwed up her face in disgust. "Animal products! Yuck! But I'll still see you at the game later, right?"

Bryn nodded. "You bet! I'll be there with bells on, or should I say *skates* on." Kelsey smiled at his terrible joke and he hardly felt guilty at all about his little lie.

***

Bryn's piano practice had gone well. The Beethoven had been the right choice. He'd stayed a little longer than he had meant to and now he had to hustle through supper in order to get to the rink on time.

"Dad, I forgot I have a game tonight. It's at eight o'clock at the Haysboro Rink. Could you give me a ride?" Bryn asked as he wolfed down his chili.

"I never thought I'd be saying this, but *both* my sons have a game tonight and Evan already asked me to drive him." His dad reached for the salad. "I think if you ask her nicely, your mom could probably drive you."

Bryn stopped in mid-chew. If his mom drove him, she'd stay and watch the game.

"Oh dear, we have a problem," his mom interrupted. "Actually, Thomas, I can't tonight. I have some work that must be finished before court tomorrow. It's my first big case and I want to be super-prepared." She turned to Bryn. "Honey, I feel terrible about this."

Thomas Selkirk smiled and patted his wife's hand. "Don't worry, Julianne. We Selkirk men are a resourceful lot." He pointed at Bryn with his fork. "I'll drop Bryn at his game early and continue on with Evan." He moved the fork in Evan's direction. "The games both start at eight which means they'll end at about the same time. Bryn will just have to wait to be picked up. Okay with you guys?"

Bryn sighed with relief. "Works fine for me, Dad." He felt like he'd dodged the bullet again.

Evan didn't look happy about the new arrangements. He dropped his fork noisily on his plate. "Hey

Bryn, some *girl* phoned for you this afternoon and said she'd gone to the Burger Barn where you were supposed to have a *part-time job,* and they'd never heard of you. You, working at a lame, nowhere job like Burger Barn? What's up with that?" Evan asked innocently, but Bryn saw the smug look on his face. Busted!

Bryn was surprised Kelsey had gone to the Burger Barn. "That was a girl from school," he explained. "And she misunderstood what I said. I'll straighten it out with her tonight." He quickly finished his meal and left the table before anyone else could ask him about his phantom job.

★★★

When Bryn's dad dropped him off at the rink, Kelsey was waiting impatiently for him.

"Hi, how's your day going?" Her voice was calm, but Bryn knew from the way she stood with her arms folded that she was ticked off.

"Hi, Kelsey." He decided he would have to do a pre-emptive strike—lie first and lie fast. He really had no choice. Besides, what was one more after all the lies he'd told? "Just the person I was looking for. I need to talk to you about something in strictest confidence." He glanced furtively around as though looking for a hidden surveillance camera. "The darndest thing happened when I went to start my new job today. It seems you have to live in Alberta for six months before the Burger Barn can hire you, but the manager took pity on me. He said I could work there, but I'd have to stay in the back and no one must know he hired me, which would get him in trouble. He's a very nice man with six children and a sick wife to support. He would lose his job if anyone found out, so of course I promised I wouldn't tell a soul. Besides my parents, you're the only one who knows about my secret job." He laid his hand on Kelsey's shoulder. "Can I count on you to keep my secret, *our* secret?"

Kelsey's eyes went wide. "No kidding? I've never heard of that before, but what would you expect from a place that serves dead animal flesh to innocent children." She made a face, then nodded in agreement. "Of course I'll keep quiet and Bryn, thanks for trusting me with such an important secret."

He felt another ton of guilt press down on him. He wasn't sure if he could hold up under the weight of all his lies.

***

Bryn still spent a lot of time sitting on the bench, but Coach Coles tried to be fair and send him out as much as possible.

"The problem is you are inconsistent, Bryn. At practice, you play well and then it comes to a real game and you can barely move the puck down the ice. It makes it tough for me to know whether you're having a good night or a bad one. Can you figure out why you play this way?"

"Honest, Coach. I really try during games. I focus on everything Lucas has taught me and I don't let my mind wander at all." Bryn couldn't tell the coach about his music; besides, he wouldn't allow the music to play while he was concentrating on a game.

The game was pretty evenly matched and both teams had to work hard for every goal. The Comets had changed strategy several times to shake up the Hornets defence, but the other team adapted quickly and were hard to beat. The Hornets' goalie was hot tonight, blocking shot after shot.

The clock was ticking down the closing minutes of the third period. The score was tied three-all. Bryn couldn't believe it when Lucas nodded at him. "You're with me on the next line change, Bryn."

"Me? But we need a super player out there right now, not a second-stringer." He looked down at his skates and tapped the blades with his stick.

"We need someone who's going to fight for our team and do his best to win. That's you." Lucas flipped his face-guard down. "You haven't been skating as much as these other guys so you've still got the fresh strength to pull this one out of the bag. Come on, we'll show these wimps what Comets can do."

Bryn climbed over the boards. They would use a play they had practised earlier. Lucas would grab the puck, pass it to Zach, their right defenceman, who would slide to the far side of the rink then pass up ice to Aaron, the other defenceman, who would smoke one to Lucas who was waiting to take the puck home. Bryn, acting as the other forward, would back him up and take the rebound, should there be one.

The second the puck dropped, Bryn gritted his teeth and concentrated. Lucas won the faceoff. He slid the puck back off his stick to Zach who spun around looking for Aaron who was waiting exactly where he was supposed to be.

Lucas, who had skated hard for his designated spot, turned to wait for his pass. The Hornets' defence was well behind the play and it looked like a great scoring chance.

Bryn couldn't skate as fast as Lucas, and had to hustle. He'd nearly caught up with the Comets' captain, when, out of the corner of his eye, he saw Aaron fire his pass. For a split second, Bryn's concentration was focused entirely on Aaron.

He never saw the rough patch of ice.

The toe of his blade caught the gouge in the ice and the next thing Bryn knew he was heading face first to the slick, glassy surface.

With a bone-jarring thump, he collided with Lucas, knocking his teammate's legs out from under him. Bryn had been skating hard and his momentum kept him sliding over the polished ice. In the next instant, he saw the surprised face of the Hornets' goalie as Bryn careened into him and the net.

The horn sounded, ending the game. The crowd started cheering and Bryn wondered what had happened. Then he saw it. Under him, wedged against his stick, was the puck. He had scored his first goal ever! The Comets had won!

Bryn squirmed out of the goal crease and tried to push himself up on his hands. His left wrist screamed with pain and a wave of nausea flooded his stomach. His wrist gave out as he fell back onto the ice.

Coach Coles and Lucas were heading toward him as he slowly got to his feet using his right hand.

"I think I've done something to my wrist," Bryn said through clenched teeth.

"Let's get you to the dressing room." Coach Coles helped Bryn off the ice as Lucas followed carrying Bryn's stick.

Kelsey was waiting at the dressing-room door. She looked pale and worried. "Are you alright?" She looked at Bryn's arm, which he held gingerly against his chest.

"Nothing to worry about. It's just a flesh wound." His lip curled into a smile. He'd always wanted to say that.

"You were great. Not the usual way to score a goal, but it worked." She laid her hand gently on Bryn's arm.

Her voice was soft and Bryn instantly felt better.

After the coach looked at his wrist, he applied an ice pack and a sling to support the arm. "You have a mild sprain. Just keep it iced for a couple of days and try not to re-injure it."

Bryn nodded. The ice felt good on the throbbing pain.

Suddenly, his dad came hurrying into the dressing room. "Bryn, are you okay?" He took in the ice pack and sling the coach had rigged for his wrist.

"Coach says it's just a minor sprain. I think I fell on it wrong." Bryn grimaced.

"Maybe we should go to the clinic and have that checked." His dad was frowning at the sling and ice.

"Honestly, Mr. Selkirk, I've seen a lot of bumps and bruises and this one's not serious." Coach Coles stuck out his hand. "Bob Coles, coach of the Comets."

"Thomas Selkirk." The men shook hands. "Thanks for looking after Bryn." He smiled. "And for turning him into a hockey player. I was just telling my wife, I never thought both—"

Bryn cut his dad off. "Hey Dad, could you help me with my skates? I'm starting to feel a little sick to my stomach, must be some kind of aftershock."

His dad stooped to unlace Bryn's skates. "Sure, no problem son."

Bryn glanced up and saw Evan standing out in the hallway with one of the rink officials. He swallowed hard as he stole a glance at Kelsey to see if she'd noticed Evan waiting.

The official walked into the dressing room, leaving Bryn's brother standing in the hallway. "Excuse me gents, but there's a young Indian fellow who says his father's in here..."

"Oh that's my—" Bryn's dad began.

"Ow, ow, ow! My wrist is killing me. I may pass out!" Bryn yowled, interrupting his dad.

His dad looked concerned. "We'd better get you home."

Kelsey, who'd been standing quietly off to one side, came forward and sat beside Bryn. "I hope you feel better soon. I'll see you tomorrow at school." She patted his good hand, then stood up and left.

Bryn felt relieved when he saw her walk past Evan without talking to him.

Soon, Bryn was changed and they were making their way to the van." So why were you here at the rink, Dad?" he asked, clambering awkwardly into the van. "I thought you were at Evan's game and would be late."

"There was a problem with the other team. They refused to play the Nighthawks and ended up forfeiting the game. We drove back to watch you play and," his dad added with a proud smile, "score your first goal in minor hockey. Great job. You got the winning goal for the Comets. Not too shabby for a rookie."

Bryn smiled sheepishly. "It wasn't exactly my great

hockey skills that got that goal, Dad."

"No, it was more like your great *curling* skills," Evan added sarcastically. "You went into that net like a winning rock in a bonspiel." He turned and looked out the van window for the rest of the ride home and Bryn wondered what was eating him.

When they arrived home, Bryn's mother was very concerned, but after assurances from his dad that it wasn't serious, everyone was allowed to relax. Not long after, Bryn and Evan went up to their rooms to get ready for bed.

Bryn was figuring out how he could undress without making his wrist hurt, when Evan came into his room.

"You really are a hypocrite," Evan began, flopping down on the bed.

Bryn was tired and his wrist was pounding. "What are you blabbering on about now, loser?"

"Don't pull that crap with me, Bryn. I've got you figured out and it's not shaping up to be a very nice picture." Evan sat back with his hands behind his head. "I saw that act tonight when I was standing in the hallway. As soon as that old guy said there was an *Indian* kid looking for his dad, your face went pale and you started howling like an idiot to distract everyone. Nice. You think I don't know what that means? Your hockey buddies don't know you're half Cree and my showing up would have blown your cover. Bryn, that stinks."

Bryn swallowed hard. He didn't know what to say.

"Next," Evan went on relentlessly, "I know you haven't told that girl about your piano. That explains her thinking you're at the Burger Barn working your fingers to the bone flipping burgers when you're actually at school practising for a killer music recital."

"Her name is Kelsey and she's a nice girl." Bryn couldn't believe how lame he sounded.

Evan was on a roll and couldn't be stopped. "And the worst thing of all. You're only *playing at* hockey, the game I love, because you want to impress *Kelsey,* and you seem to be willing to risk an awful lot to be on that team." He nodded at Bryn's sling. "You preached at me about throwing away my future and here you are with a sprained wrist a month before a major piano competition! Are you brain-dead?"

He stood up. "I saw you play tonight. Despite the fluky goal, not your best effort, and I know why, too." He ran his hand through his hair. "Look, I just find it incredible that you'd rather hide the truth about your family like you're ashamed of us and play second-, no, fifth-rate hockey and maybe ruin your piano career forever than tell this Kelsey the truth. Do you really want to be friends with her if she doesn't want you for who you are? Bryn, you're a kid with a white father and an Indian mother and your greatest talent is that you play wicked piano." He turned to leave then stopped. "And the next time you start yelling at me about my friends and my future, take a look in the mirror first."

Evan slammed the door so hard Bryn's picture of Beethoven with the fake autograph fell off the wall. He walked slowly over to the picture and hung it back up. Evan just didn't understand. How could he? He's always been a loner and never had any friends, especially not a girlfriend.

Bryn sat on his bed. So what if he was stretching things a little? He'd straighten it all out soon.

11 SOMETIMES A LIE IS A GUY'S BEST FRIEND

Christmas was not fun that year. Bryn and Evan fought constantly and their parents were often drawn in to break up any particularly loud arguments.

After Christmas, Bryn was kept busy perfecting his piano piece for the recital and getting ready for the big tournament during Minor Hockey Week. He still hadn't told Kelsey about the piano contest and, since it was in Edmonton, which was three hours away by car, maybe he could continue to keep it a secret.

Evan had been hanging out with Craig and his hockey buddies every chance he got. He said his friends were cool, but he did find himself defending them a lot, both on the ice and off. The Nighthawks' tactics on the rink were getting them bad publicity and a lot of teams were complaining. Craig said they were all a bunch of whiners; the Nighthawks got results, didn't they?

At home, neither twin spoke to the other much; they had nothing to say.

★★★

The Comets were on a hot streak. Bryn and his team were gearing up for Minor Hockey Week. The team had decided that this year the Comets were going to claim the championship. The team had been squeezing in extra practices and Bryn was being stretched to his limits. It was exhausting. Kelsey had told him she was proud of the way he *tried.* He would have liked it better if she had said she liked the way he *played so well,* but that wouldn't have been true; when it came to real games, he played dismally. The truth was his playing was getting even worse as he became increasingly tired from his busy schedule of piano and hockey.

"Our shot at the championship is all because of you, Lucas," Bryn said after the Comets' latest win, in which Bryn had very little part. The team was enjoying hamburgers and fries at a local restaurant, courtesy of Coach Coles. "You really are the greatest player in the league."

Lucas looked embarrassed. "Craig Carpenter from the Nighthawks has the highest points, not me," he reminded Bryn.

"Yeah, but they're all dirty points from his goon-squad tactics," Kelsey added, sipping her soda.

Just then, Jordan Cairn sat down next to Bryn. He looked even smaller when he was out of his bulky uniform. Bryn had heard that the tiny goalie had really bad asthma, but Jordan never let it stop him playing.

"Hey, what's with that Indian kid the Nighthawks picked up this season?" Jordan asked. "He's kind of a mystery man. He never has a name on his jersey, just his number."

Bryn stared down at his hamburger as if there were a secret message written on the bun.

"I'm not sure what his name is, Seldon or Smith, something like that." Lucas said, shaking his head.

"Whatever his name is, number 07 is every goalie's worst nightmare. When I see him start his run, I hunker down and hold on." Jordan took a huge bite of his burger.

"Speaking of getting goalies to shake in their skates," Lucas began. "We're going to stay with the extra practices. This year, on Saturday, January 20th, the Comets' name is going on that championship cup."

Bryn swallowed. He already had piano practice every night and had cut a couple short so he could go to hockey. He wasn't sure how he was going to continue to be in two places at once, but somehow he would have to do it.

***

When Bryn lied to Mr. Boothby to get out of two more piano practices that week, he knew he was skating on thin ice. He was heading for a major penalty if the old teacher ever found out. He made sure Lucas took his equipment to the rink so Mr. Boothby wouldn't see him with it and get suspicious.

"Mr. Selkirk!" Mr. Boothby's voice echoed down the hallway at school. "I need to speak to you! *Now*!"

Bryn stopped in his tracks as he felt his stomach turn over. He had a bad feeling about this. Taking a deep breath, he followed his teacher into the office.

Mr. Boothby turned to him, a grim look on his weathered face. "I don't want any more lies, young man. Did you really think I wouldn't know what you've been up to? I want you to choose right now, right here—hockey or piano. I'm not wasting my time on someone who does not have his priorities straight." The angry teacher stood silently waiting for an answer.

Bryn knew he had no choice. He had to lie again. "I'm sorry about this week, Mr. Boothby. If you will give me one more chance, I'll give up hockey. I'm not a very good player anyway, and besides, piano is number one in my life." The last part, at least, was true.

This seemed to satisfy his music teacher. "That's a wise decision, Mr. Selkirk. I think you've indulged this foolishness for long enough. I expect you to make up the practices you've missed this week. I'll leave it up to you to figure out how. You are dismissed."

Bryn left the office feeling worse than ever. He couldn't fit in regular practices now. How was he going to make up two extra?

When he got home that night, his parents had gone

out and he was alone with Evan. After practising his piano for an hour with very unsatisfactory results, he wandered into the family room where Evan was playing a video game on the computer.

"I'm going to get something to eat. Do you want anything?" he asked. He was so tired, he momentarily forgot they were feuding.

"I'm not hungry," Evan said curtly without turning away from the screen

Bryn was just about to leave when Evan stopped and looked over at him. "Hey, Bryn," he said in an oddly quiet voice. "Thanks for asking."

Bryn shrugged and left the family room. He grabbed a cheese and cucumber sandwich and went up to his room. Lying on his bed, eating his sandwich, he tried to figure a way out of the mess he'd tangled himself into. He was so tired. How was he ever going to have the strength to get through this?

"Your playing sucks." Evan's voice startled Bryn. He was leaning against the doorjamb.

Bryn wasn't sure which he meant—hockey or piano. "Thanks for the vote of confidence." He put his arm across his eyes and willed his nosy brother to disappear.

"Look, I don't care what you do with your sorry life, but I do care about hockey. You should face one cold, hard fact Bryn. You are *never* going to play great hockey." He shook his head. "But you *are* a born natural on the piano. You make it look easy. Hockey...not such a pretty picture when you're out on the ice. I can't help you with the piano, but I can tell you how you can improve your game so it's not so painful to watch." Evan came into Bryn's room and slouched into a chair.

"If you're going to tell me I need to practise, you're right. I just can't find enough hours in the day. Honest Evan, I really *like* hockey," he smiled at his brother, not a big hearty smile, more of a twitch of the corners of his mouth, but it was a start. "It's just that I *love* playing piano. But Kelsey is really into hockey and, well, she's pretty cool." He felt foolish talking to his brother like this.

"Will you quit babbling for a minute so I can talk?" Evan said.

Bryn sat up, dusting the sandwich crumbs off his shirt. "Okay, I'm listening."

"That's what you should do when you're in a game situation," Evan said cryptically.

Bryn's face must have looked confused because Evan gave him an exasperated look. "You need to listen to that crazy music you always have going in your head. Pick a song that rocks and skate your way to fame and fortune. Haven't you noticed you skate better and stick-handle pretty decently when you listen to your music?"

Bryn still looked unsure and Evan sighed. "I watched you play in a game, remember. As soon as you stopped listening to your tunes, your head stopped bopping up and down and your skating went into the toilet. First, last, and always, you're a musician, Bryn. Turn the music back on." Without another word, he got up and left.

Bryn was stunned. First, because this was the only conversation in months he and Evan had had where they weren't at each others throats. And stranger than that, Evan had told him something to help his hockey! Bryn thought about what Evan had said. He had purposefully turned the music off so he could concentrate on his game. Had he been wrong? Maybe Evan was right. That would account for his inconsistent playing between practices and games. Maybe he should just turn up the volume and go along for the ride. What did he have to lose? All of a sudden, he was actually looking forward to the tournament.

12 PIZZA AND PUCKS

Minor Hockey Week would begin on Saturday. Evan and his Nighthawks buddies were sure the cup was in the bag. There had been another incident at the mall, so the boys decided to lie low at Evan's house until the security guard had a chance to cool off.

Evan knew his mom was working late again and his dad was driving Bryn from piano to hockey, so he wasn't surprised when he saw a note instructing him to order a pizza. His dad had left his credit card for Evan to use.

Evan thought briefly about how much money he had spent lately and was glad his dad had left his card.

"Man, your dad leaves you his plastic to order pizza? Must be nice." Craig shook his head.

"What's so strange about that? It's not like I'm going to go to Vegas with his card." Evan led the boys to the family room where Craig immediately headed over to the computer.

"Do you have Internet access?" Craig asked, sitting down at the keyboard.

"Sure, why?" Evan wondered what Craig was up to now.

"You've got to check out this hockey equipment site I found. It's unbelievable." Craig quickly typed in the correct name and, as the four boys watched, the screen suddenly came to life. The site had to be every hockey player's number-one pick. There were pages of the latest equipment, clothes, and accessories, ready to be ordered with the click of a mouse.

When the pizza arrived, Evan signed for it and tossed the credit card and receipt on the hall table. They all helped themselves to the deep dish, stuffed crust pizza with four kinds of meat. For the next hour they ate and went through the site for the sixth time, deciding on what equipment they'd order if they ever became millionaires.

"This is unbelievable," Trevor said with his mouth full. "I think I could run up a four-digit bill pretty quickly from this place. They have everything."

"And they deliver," Jamie added with a grin, showing where one of his front teeth was missing.

"If I were king of the world, I'd order myself a complete equipment overhaul. First class all the way," Craig said scrolling through screen after screen of the pricey equipment.

"Your birthday's in March, Craig. Maybe you can get your parents to give you an early present," Evan suggested, watching the screen as it displayed a whole page of top of the line biaxial design kneepads.

"I won't be holding my breath on that one," Craig said, a distinct iciness in his voice.

"Who knows? It never hurts to ask," Evan joked, feeling a little uncomfortable at Craig's sudden change of tone.

"Look, my world sure isn't the same as yours with your fancy house and credit cards and doting parents. I don't know where my dad is, he left a long time ago, and I never see my mom for longer than it takes for her to yell at me to get out of her sight, so I don't think I'll be getting any special present from her in the near future." Craig stood up, stalked over to the table, and grabbed the last piece of pizza.

"Hey, I'm sorry, Craig. I didn't know," Evan said trying to apologize.

Craig looked at the pictures on the wall above the table. They showed scenes of Evan and his family up north, skating, snowmobiling, and sledding. The one of Evan and his dad holding up two large fish they had just caught seemed to hold Craig's attention. "Before my dad cut out, we used to go fishing. I remember sticking the hook through the worm and worrying it was hurting the stupid thing." He shook his head. "I was so dumb then."

"Do you ever see your dad now?" Evan asked.

Craig flinched. "Who knows? It's been so long I could pass him on the street and I wouldn't recognize him." He looked around the room. "You've got it made, Selkirk. Cutesy family, brains, and you can even play passable hockey." He shrugged his shoulders as though sloughing off any thoughts of his own less-than-perfect family life.

Evan watched him walk back over to the computer. It had never occurred to Evan that he had a life someone else might actually envy. He wondered if Craig missed his dad.

Later, after the guys had left, Evan cleaned up the pizza mess. He was still thinking about Craig as he stuffed the empty boxes into a big black garbage bag. He noticed absently that the credit card was still sitting by itself on the hallway table. He'd spent more on the pizzas than he should have and hoped his dad wouldn't be mad. His parents had been angry with him a lot lately and it was getting a little depressing. Evan looked for the receipt to show his dad how much the total bill had been, but he couldn't find it. It must have been thrown out with the trash when he was cleaning up.

★★★

It was the last game before the championships began and the Nighthawks were going for a win. They were playing the Carredale Kings and they were going to be tough to beat.

"Pass me the puck and I'll show this goalie wannabe

what the Nighthawks can do!" Craig yelled at Tank Gowan, who was skating hard toward the Kings' goal.

"Too much traffic,"Tank called, as he deked around one of the Kings' forwards.

"Don't argue, Gowan. Pass me the puck!" Craig snarled through his face guard. With a curse, Tank flipped a forward pass, but the Kings player stuck out his stick and deflected the puck. Craig cursed Tank for his sloppy effort.

Evan saw what had happened and moved up to get the speeding puck. He turned and started for the Kings' net. Out of the corner of his eye, he could see Craig on his left. Evan knew Craig would try to strip the puck from him. For some reason, this idea really bugged him. He wanted to finish with as many points as possible and he wasn't about to give any to Craig.

He put on a burst of speed and started his run at the goal. The goalie was out of his net, effectively cutting down the angles. As Evan got closer, the goalie moved smoothly back into the crease making an open target much harder to find. Ahead, the two defenceman set up a screen.

Evan shook his head. Like he was going to let these guys spoil his scoring chance! He skated straight for the first Kings player. He hit the defenceman hard, knocking him out of his way.

Craig was close enough to the other defenceman; he could have taken him out, leaving Evan a clear run at the goalie. Instead, Craig hung back, forcing Evan to take the second skater out as well.

The other Kings defenceman was ready. Without his forward momentum, Evan couldn't bump the big skater away from the goalmouth. Evan cursed under his breath. He was so close to the net he could see the colour of the goalie's eyes, but he couldn't get a clear shot. Looking around for help, Evan knew he had no choice. He used a backhand pass to get the puck to Craig, who was waiting behind the play.

Craig scooped the puck, sped around the net and slammed in a nice wraparound. The game was tied. The Nighthawks needed only one goal to finish with a win.

"Man, you Nighthawks really know how to play as a team," the big defenceman who was still tangled up with Evan said sarcastically. "Maybe you need a little lesson," he snarled. Screening himself from the ref's view, the big defenceman butt-ended Evan in the stomach. Evan gasped, then saw red. Before he could stop himself, he pulled his gloved fist back and slammed it into the guy's face mask.

The big defenceman snickered as he dropped to the ice. "That will cost you." He grabbed his head as though Evan's punch had seriously hurt him.

Before he could say a word, whistles were shrilling and linesmen surrounded Evan. Glaring at the creep, Evan headed for the penalty box.

Being short-handed turned into a disaster for the

Nighthawks when the Kings pulled their goalie and put an extra forward on the ice. Paco couldn't stop the rush and the Kings were up by one goal. Unfortunately, it turned out to be the winning goal. The Nighthawks lost the game, but they were far enough ahead in league points that they held on to first place. Craig didn't speak to Evan as they got changed later. Evan was so angry he didn't care.

On the ride home he wondered why he was so angry. Sure Craig was playing like a jerk, but he always played that way. Taking a penalty wasn't such a big deal, except he had really wanted to hurt the guy. He shuddered with a sudden chill. He was turning into a true Nighthawk.

13 SUBSTITUTE PLAYER ON THE HOME TEAM

Bryn's piano practice was terrible.

"Mr. Selkirk, your playing is abysmal. Are you ill?" Mr. Boothby's shaggy eyebrows went up with concern.

Bryn had to go to yet another hockey practice and jumped at this handy excuse, "Actually, I am feeling really crummy. Maybe we should cut piano short today."

Mr. Boothby shook his head. "We have very little time left, Mr. Selkirk. The competition is this weekend and the calibre of playing will be extremely high. You need to be in top form."

"I know it will be tough and that's why I should go home now and rest to recharge my batteries." Bryn gathered up his sheet music and left without another word. Lucas had taken his equipment to the rink so all Bryn had to do was get over there. He promised himself he would practise his piano when he got home no matter how tired he was.

At hockey practice, Bryn always left the music on in his head. He was looking forward to trying out

Evan's suggestion in a real game situation. Today though, nothing seemed to help. He was so tired he could barely hold up his hockey stick.

"You better go home and get some sleep, Bryn, or you'll be no help to the Comets on the weekend," Lucas said, skating over and patting Bryn on the shoulder.

At the mention of the weekend, Bryn winced inside. Everything was such a mess.

Bryn dragged himself home, dreading the idea that he had to practise on the piano for at least an hour before he went to bed tonight. He was having a little trouble with one passage and he wanted it perfect. He had always loved practising, but now the thought of it made him groan.

He trudged home through the snow; his equipment bag weighed a ton on his back. The arena was only a few blocks from his house, but it felt like kilometres. He was crossing an intersection when the glare from an approaching car made him look up. Quickly, he ducked his head inside his parka hood and hunched over. It was Mr. Boothby's old green station wagon! Bryn was caught in the headlight beams like a startled deer on the highway. He hustled across the crosswalk and down the street, desperately hoping old Boothby's night sight wasn't very good and he hadn't recognized Bryn.

Finally, still vibrating from his near miss, Bryn made it home to find Evan watching TV in the family room.

"Mom and Dad will be home soon, so don't eat

anything," Evan instructed without looking up.

"Whatever," Bryn mumbled as he started up the stairs for a hot bath. He ached everywhere. He had just made it to the top stair when he heard the telephone ring. Bryn knew that Evan would never tear himself away from his show to answer the phone, but there was no way he could trudge back downstairs to get the call, it was just too painful. Bryn decided to let the machine pick it up.

Suddenly he heard a familiar voice on the answering machine. "I'm calling for the parents of Bryn Selkirk. It's Mr. Boothby, his piano instructor."

Bryn spun around and hustled back downstairs, panic fuelling his tired muscles. He ran into the family room in time to see Evan scramble for the phone.

"Hello, Mr. Boothby," Evan said in a low growling baritone. "This is Thomas Selkirk, Bryn's father. Is there a problem?" He listened for a moment, then nodded. "I see, hockey you say, and a girl!" Evan's eyebrows went up in mock surprise. "Well, this is serious. Let me have a talk with the boy." Evan looked over at Bryn and held his thumb up in a sign everything was going to be all right. "Yes, I know the competition is this weekend. I'm sure that after I have a *serious* and *stern* talk with him he will come to see the error of his ways and you can forget this incident." His mouth was twisting into a grin and Bryn knew he was going to lose it in a moment. "Absolutely no more *tomfoolery.* Thank you for calling, Mr. Boothby, and goodbye." The second he replaced the phone, Evan began laughing.

"What's so funny?" Bryn asked, feeling indignant at being the butt of Evan's stupid joke. "This means Mr. Boothby busted me for going to hockey tonight. When Mom and Dad find out, I'm going to be in big trouble." He sat down on the couch with a thump. "Man, will this ever end?"

Evan calmed down, pushing his hair back off his forehead in an old and familiar gesture Bryn hadn't seen for a while.

"You bonehead! Your dad already knows and will speak to you about it." He lowered his voice in his pitiful imitation of their father. *"And everything will be hunky dory!"*

"Oh," was all Bryn could think of to say for a moment. Then his face broke into a slow grin as he realized what Evan had done for him. "Oh yeah! Cool! Thanks, Evan!" He thought about what this would mean. He would have to make sure Mr. Boothby never got the chance to talk to his dad about their little phone conversation. "This means I now have no place on earth where my life doesn't consist of piles of dog crap which I have to tap dance around to keep from stepping right in it."

"Consider this my good deed for the next year. Just keep it in mind in case I ever need the favour returned." Evan shook his head. "Bryn, you realize you're playing with fire here. I don't just mean the lies. Do you remember how you hurt your wrist a while back? What if it had been serious and you could never play the piano again? It could happen. Sports injuries put guys out of action permanently all the time. All I'm saying is think about it. I guess it comes down to making the right choices." Turning, he went back to the television.

Bryn walked slowly back upstairs. He felt confused. It wasn't like Evan to go out on a limb to help anyone, and when had his brother become such a know-it-all about making right choices?

However, the bigger question remained unasked. Was he right?

★★★

It was getting to be so crazy, Bryn couldn't keep all the lies straight. He'd told everyone so many different stories; he wasn't sure what he'd told whom.

"Are you ready to win a championship this weekend?" Kelsey asked as they walked to class.

Bryn had to stop for a moment to make sure he said the right thing. After that close call with Mr. Boothby, he'd worked everything out. Timing was crucial, but with a little luck, he could pull it off. During the week all the various teams would play against one another, and then the championship game between the top two teams was Saturday morning. He would spend the week scrambling frantically between piano practice and playing hockey. After the game Saturday morning he would pretend to be feeling sick and tell Kelsey he wouldn't be going to the banquet that night. At this point, he and his parents would drive up to Edmonton in the afternoon and meet Mr. Boothby for the piano recital Saturday evening. Simple!

Bryn nodded. "Saturday will be a day the Comets and I will always remember," he said, trying to sound confident.

Kelsey nodded enthusiastically. "Lucas is sure the Comets are going to go for the gold this year." She hesitated. "Have you thought about the big wrap-up dance and banquet?" She smiled at him rather shyly. "I am *so* looking forward to that. I'm doing the new dress and hairdo thing this year, a first for me." She began to fidget with her textbook. "I was hoping you would want to sit with me, I mean, my family and your family could sit together at the banquet, unless you don't want to." She looked at him expectantly.

Bryn didn't know what to say. A banquet and a dance where all the players and *their families* would be together! It was a good thing he was going to be sick.

"Ah, sure. We can sit together, of course, who else would I sit with?" He tried to smile at her, but inside he felt like he was going to fly apart. He'd been so careful juggling everything, keeping all his balls in the air so none hit the ground and exploded in his face. Now he was going to have to not only lie to Kelsey, but disappoint her in what was obviously a big thing to her. If she found out about his ditching the banquet to play the piano, he was dead meat. To pull this one off he had no choice but to continue his career as the world's biggest liar.

14 HOME TEAM ADVANTAGE

Minor Hockey Week was a blast. Everyone was playing great hockey and the battle for first was heating up.

Finally it was Friday and the two top teams were announced. It was going to be the Nighthawks against the Comets.

Evan chuckled to himself as he walked into the pizza restaurant where he was meeting Craig and the guys after school. The idea that he would be playing against his brother in a championship hockey game was not something he would have bet on a couple of months ago. Their dad would be walking on air with two sons playing for the championship. The Selkirks would end up winners whichever team came out on top.

"I know we can beat those Comet hacks," Jamie laughed, grabbing the last piece of pepperoni pizza.

"Yeah, I'm not worried. The only player who could cause us trouble is Lucas Coles, he's good." Craig looked thoughtful. "In fact, he's *too* good. If Coles couldn't play, for whatever reason," he paused for effect, "like someone checking him so hard that he's out of the game permanently, then I know the Comets would fall apart. Look at that rookie player they put on the ice every game. That guy's just a speed bump on skates," he laughed.

Evan frowned. He thought about how far Bryn had come in such a short time. Lucas Coles had to be a great guy and an even greater coach to turn Bryn into any kind of a hockey player. Even if Bryn wasn't first string, Lucas had done wonders with him in a very short time.

Evan suddenly didn't like the way everyone was looking at him. "You're not serious about taking Lucas out of the game? I'm here to play hockey, not hurt some guy who's just out there doing his job."

Craig scowled and tossed his crust down on his plate. "I remember when you signed on, Selkirk. You said you had no problem with using muscle." He looked hard at Evan. "You've done such a great job since you've been with us, I would have thought you'd jump at the chance to punch Coles a one-way ticket to the dressing room." He laughed again, then reached over and grabbed the last piece of pizza away from Jamie, stuffing it into his mouth.

Evan felt nervous. Craig was crazy enough to *really* hurt Lucas. The truth was the Nighthawks were a good hockey team even without the strong-arm stuff.

Evan was sure they could win without the blood and bruises.

As Evan returned home, he was still worrying whether Craig was serious when he said he'd wanted Lucas Coles hurt. Craig's definition of "hurt" scared Evan.

As he hung up his jacket, he became aware of raised voices in the living room and wondered what all the yelling was about. Maybe Bryn's crazy old piano teacher had called back and spilled the beans about the phoney call.

Evan walked into a scene from a hockey player's wish book. There were boxes and cartons everywhere and they were filled with every type of hockey equipment imaginable. There were Jofa elbow pads, Hespeler gloves, Bauer shin and shoulder pads, as well as top of the line Bauer skates, and Nike hockey pants. A new Koho stick and blade lay on the couch.

"Wow! Look at all this stuff," he said, whistling appreciatively. His mother was standing with her arms crossed as his dad paced up and down the living room.

His dad whirled on him. "Evan, what in heaven's name was running through your mind? Who gave you permission to order this equipment and use my credit card?"

Evan was speechless. He didn't know what his dad was talking about. Then he spotted the invoice on the table next to a shining new Hi-Tech helmet.

He picked up the invoice and scanned it. There was a thousand dollars' worth of equipment listed! The order had been placed over the Internet to the site he and his friends had checked out that night they had ordered pizza. A cold feeling gripped Evan's stomach.

The pizza order with his dad's credit card! He remembered when he was cleaning up he couldn't find the receipt. He had thought he must have thrown it out with the rest of the trash, but obviously someone picked it up and used the card number to order all this equipment.

That someone could only be Craig Carpenter. He must have done this as some kind of stupid joke. "Dad, it wasn't me," Evan began in his own defence.

"If this was one of your juvenile delinquent friends, so help me Evan, I'm going to call the police. I've put up with you skipping school, calls from the principal, late nights, bad language, dropping grades and I suspect a host of trouble I know nothing about, but this..." He waved his arm indicating all the boxes. "This is the last straw. I don't know what has happened to you since we moved here, but both your mother and I are very worried about your behaviour." He ran his hand through his hair very much like Evan always did.

"We've talked about it and think that perhaps sending you to a private school where you will receive stricter supervision might get you back on track. It would be for your own good. If you keep going the way you're headed, you'll end up in young offenders' court as a defendant instead of a lawyer."

Evan didn't know what to say. He felt real panic well

up inside him. If he said it was Craig, his dad would call the police, but if he took the blame he would end up in some military school where it was all spit and polish. This time he was in a corner and didn't know how to get out.

There was a sudden movement at the door. All eyes turned toward Bryn, who stood silently watching the scene.

"I'm sorry I forgot to give this to Dad, Evan," he said holding out an envelope. "I know you said wait until we knew how much was on the invoice, but I was listening to some music when the delivery arrived and..." He handed his father the envelope.

Evan's dad opened the envelope and looked inside, then he looked at Evan. "There's one thousand dollars cash in here. Am I to believe you planned on paying for this equipment yourself?" His eyebrows went up in surprise.

"Yeah, Dad," Bryn hurried on with an explanation. "Evan told me he had no other way of ordering the equipment, and it was such a great buy he couldn't pass it up. He saved a lot by ordering it on sale through the Internet."

"It seems like a big expenditure, Thomas," Evan's mom said reaching for the envelope, "but the money in his savings account is his, and the way he's growing, we would have had to buy new equipment next year anyway. If Evan was able to get these things at a good price, then he did well to think ahead." She sighed. "I just thought we had agreed the money would be for his education."

Evan held his breath as he frantically tried to come up with an answer that would satisfy his mom and dad. He looked over at Bryn for help.

Bryn never missed a beat. "No worries, Mom. He's going to begin saving regularly and replace the money in his account. Starting right away, he's going to get an after-school job at the Burger Barn."

Evan jumped in to back up his brother's wild story. "That's absolutely correct. I thought about the way things have been going lately. I've screwed up, but that's all over now. I think my adjustment period to the big city is over. I figured that if I worked harder at school and brought my grades back up, then you wouldn't mind if I got a job. I was going to talk to you about it before the shipment arrived, but they sent it sooner than I expected." Evan figured if he was going to back his brother up, there was no sense skimping on the embellishments. Then the whole crazy thing hit him. The more he thought about it, the more the impossible story made sense.

His parents looked at one another.

"Apparently there was a mix-up, Thomas." Evan's mom nodded slowly. "Maybe we should give the boy the benefit of the doubt. Besides, when was the last time Bryn backed Evan up on anything? It must be the truth."

Thomas shook his head and looked at his two sons. Evan knew that look. His dad used it at school when one of the kids told a story that didn't quite ring true. This time, however, he relented. "Okay. If you promise to replace this money in your account." He held up the envelope stuffed with twenty-dollar bills.

Evan looked at Bryn with a new appreciation for his brother. "I will, I promise."

★★★

Evan busied himself putting the equipment away in the garage. He had thought about returning it, but decided he didn't want to make any more fuss about the Internet buying.

He was just finishing up when Bryn walked in. "You didn't buy that stuff, did you? I think your buddy Craig Carpenter did."

Evan sat down on a mystery box that hadn't been unpacked from their move yet. "Okay, you're right. It was Craig. I'm going to deal with him as soon as I finish here. There are a couple of things I have to talk to him about." Evan knew he was going to have to have a showdown with Craig, and suddenly, he was looking forward to it. It was about time. "Look, I know we haven't been getting along and that's at least partly my fault." He gave Bryn a sheepish look. "I also know you didn't have to do what you did today. You could have left me twisting in the wind. What you did means a lot to me, Bryn. How did you know what was going on?"

Bryn smiled. "As soon as the shipment arrived, Dad started freaking and yelling about a thousand dollars being charged on his credit card. I knew you wouldn't do that, so it had to be one of your friends trying to get you into trouble. As you know, I'm pretty good with money."

Evan rolled his eyes because for as long as he could remember Bryn had been the cheapest kid he knew. He socked away every penny he got.

"While all the fireworks were going off," Bryn went on, "I sneaked out and ran to the ATM machine at the corner store. I had five hundred in my account so I took everything out. I had the rest of the money stashed at home so I combined my entire fortune and stuck it in that envelope." He looked down at his sneakers. "I've been saving up for a new piano, but I guess the old one will do until you pay me back from your job at the Burger Barn." He looked at his brother.

Evan felt embarrassed at his brother's generosity. "Couldn't you have picked a different place? I never imagined myself as a burger baron before, but I guess it won't be so bad."

"You might even like working at—what was it you called it?—a *lame, nowhere job*," Bryn joked. "Lots of staff discounts on fries."

Evan laughed. "Yeah, Fries-R-Us. Don't worry. I'm

going to pay you back every cent as soon as possible." He took a deep breath and looked down at his hands. "Bryn, it might take a while to pay you back. I don't have any money left in my account because I've been taking it out and spending it on stupid things. I was an idiot. Is that okay?" He looked up at his brother.

Bryn smiled. "Is it okay if you're an idiot? No. Try to work on that, will you? About paying back the money, sure, I know you'll do the best you can, and you know what? Your best is pretty awesome. You'll be out of debt before you can say 'double-size fries'!"

"Thanks, Bryn, you really saved my butt." Evan looked at his brother, unable to say more.

Bryn shrugged. "No worries. Hey, if I remember correctly, I owed you one anyway."

Evan finished putting the last of the new equipment away. "Look, I've got to go straighten some stuff out. Will you tell Mom and Dad I'll be back later? I don't want to explain where I'm going."

"Sure, no problem." Bryn started back into the house, then stopped and looked at Evan. "A wise brother once told me it was all about making the right choices. You might keep that in mind."

★★★

Evan walked grimly back to the pizza restaurant where he had left his friends. They were still at the same table,

Craig slouching in the booth with the others.

"Well, look who's back? It's Selkirk, and he doesn't look happy. What's the matter, trouble in paradise?" Craig grinned, the skin on his face pulling tight and making him look like a death's head mask.

"Do you know what kind of trouble you got me into?" Evan exploded.

Craig sat up straighter from his slouch. "You got your *early birthday present*!" He scoffed nastily. "How nice. What's the matter, I thought an *Indian kid* like you would get a kick out of a little new equipment." His voice was sarcastic and Evan heard the malice in it.

"You jerk. That wasn't funny at all. I suggest you lose that credit card number and never even think about using it again. If there's one more unexplained charge on that card, I'll have no choice but to tell my dad everything and I know he'll go to the cops in a heartbeat." Evan was furious now and it took all his self-control not to punch Craig in his lying mouth.

Craig's eyes narrowed making him look even more ghoulish. "If you're not careful, Selkirk, you won't be playing in the big game tomorrow and you'll miss your chance to take out Lucas Coles for the rest of the season."

Evan saw red. "That's another mistake you made. Do you actually think I would try to hurt Lucas on purpose just so you can get some kind of sick revenge? You're so twisted you aren't thinking like a team captain anymore, just a thug on skates. The way your team is going, the Nighthawks will be suspended and none of you will play hockey again this season."

Craig stood up so quickly, his half-full soda crashed to the floor. "As long as you're playing on the Nighthawks, you'll do exactly what I say or you'll sit on the bench for the rest of the season. Am I making myself clear, Selkirk?"

Evan thought of everything that he and Craig had done the past few months. It made him feel ashamed. He realized Craig simply wasn't smart enough to figure out he was heading for disaster. Bryn had told him to make the right choice, and he now knew what that was.

"If it means listening to your poisoned plans, Craig, I would rather sit out the rest of the season in the stands than take one more order from you. You and the Nighthawks can play any kind of rotten hockey you want but this 'Indian kid' is not going to be a part of it. *I quit*!" He turned and walked away feeling better than he had in a long time.

"You'll have your walking papers tonight, Selkirk. Don't think you can come crawling back, because we don't want you!" Craig's furious shouting followed Evan out of the restaurant.

He was off the Nighthawks, but that wasn't the important thing anymore. He felt as if he'd been in a bad dream and was awake now: He was back on track. He smiled as he walked home through the cold night air.

★★★

Craig was true to his word. Later that evening, someone slipped a letter for Evan into the Selkirk mailbox. It was his release papers from the Nighthawks. He was officially no longer a player on any team in the league. He stuffed the papers into his jacket pocket in the hall closet and headed out to the garage. He'd miss hockey but not the Nighthawks.

As he finished in the garage, he thought about how fast things could change. Tomorrow was the big game and he was going to be sitting in the stands watching his brother play. School wasn't going to be the same now that he was off the Nighthawks, but somehow, he'd get by as just plain old Evan Selkirk, boy genius.

When he looked at the big picture, the cheap thrills he'd experienced hanging out with Craig and the guys really didn't stack up with his family, his future, and the way he felt about himself. He'd messed up, but tonight, he'd taken a big step toward fixing the problems he'd made.

15 SECRETS REVEALED

Bryn woke up very early the next morning. He hadn't slept well at all. This weekend was going to be like an out-of-control roller coaster ride and he had a one-way ticket.

His dad made them a big breakfast of pancakes, bacon, eggs, toast, and Cree tea. Cree tea was named after Bryn's Cree grandmother who had made tea in the same pot for as long as he could remember. She would boil the water in the old wide-mouthed kettle on the stove, then put the tea bags directly into the kettle instead of a teapot. The tea was always very hot and strong, just the way Bryn liked it.

"I wonder what's keeping your brother?" Thomas asked as he poured more pancake batter onto the skillet. "He's going to miss breakfast and he'll need all the energy he can get for playing against the mighty Comets." He smiled at his son.

Just then, Evan appeared at the kitchen door.

His mom, who was sitting at the table, looked up

and smiled. "Good morning, sweetheart. Today's the big day. My two sons will be playing in a hockey tournament together for the first time. Isn't it exciting?"

"Mom, Dad, I won't be playing today." Evan stood at the door not moving. His parents stared at him, surprised at his announcement.

Bryn looked up. "What? Why not? Don't tell me the league finally tossed out that bunch of thugs you play for?"

"No, I tossed them." Evan shuffled uncomfortably from one foot to another. "I quit last night and I had good reasons which I really don't want to go into now, if that's okay with everyone." His family sat in stunned silence.

Bryn knew what hockey meant to his brother and how this decision must have killed him. They looked at each other and a silent message passed between them. They both understood what had happened without explanations. "Sure, no problem Evan. Are you still going to come and see me play?"

Evan smiled at Bryn. "I wouldn't miss it. I want to be there when the Comets wipe up the ice with that bunch of second-raters."

This made Bryn feel better about the game today. It would probably be his last game as a Comet, because when he didn't show up for the banquet and the truth came out about his lying, he wasn't sure he could face Kelsey or the team even if they wanted him. Today, though, he was going to make his brother proud of him.

"Just remember Bryn—*turn that crazy music on*!" Evan said as he sat down to have breakfast with the rest of the family.

"I won't forget," Bryn said. He was already mentally picking his playlist.

★★★

The arena was packed when the family arrived. The game was going to be even more exciting because several head honchos from the Canadian Hockey Association were here to watch. Bryn was just saying goodbye when Kelsey and Lucas walked through the doors. His first instinct was to leave his family standing there before Kelsey saw them together. Somehow, he couldn't bring himself to do it, not after what Evan had done. Bryn was finally figuring out his own priorities and making choices he should have made a long time ago.

Kelsey looked over at them curiously, then waved tentatively. Bryn waved back, nodded to his family and started for the dressing room.

After the game, he would explain everything. If Kelsey and Lucas wanted to stay his friends, that would be great. He would understand if they didn't because he had deceived them. That was justified; he'd been wrong.

When it came to the other stuff, Evan was right. If they didn't like him for who he really was, it would never have worked anyway. Something big he now realized was that if they couldn't accept him because his mom was Cree or he was a musician, then *he* didn't want to be *their* friend. It was his turn to make some choices.

★★★

The dressing room was noisy and the energy level high. Everyone was pumped up for the game.

"Hey Bryn," Lucas called. "I have something for you."

Bryn walked over to where the tall captain stood in his dark blue uniform. "We thought a Comet who tries as hard as you do should be recognized." He reached into his equipment bag and brought out a new jersey, holding it up for Bryn to see.

Bryn looked at the Comet insignia on the front and frowned, a little confused. "That's nice, Lucas, but I have a jersey, remember?"

Lucas looked down at the uniform. "Oh, not that side, this side," he smiled and turned the shirt around.

Bryn stared, and then his face broke into a huge grin. The jersey had his number sixteen in big numerals just like his old one, but above the number sixteen, in bold letters, was the name *Selkirk*. He reached for the jersey, the one with *his* name on it. "Thanks, Lucas. This is the coolest thing I've ever seen."

"Try not to get any blood on it. The Nighthawks are going to be brutal." Lucas winked encouragingly at Bryn.

Bryn nodded and walked over to where he'd left his equipment bag. He could hardly wait to put his new uniform on. Unzipping the bag, he looked inside. Bryn couldn't believe what he saw. Instead of his old hand-me-down equipment, there were the brand new Bauer shin and shoulder pads, Jofa elbow pads with Hespeler gloves, Nike hockey pants, and a High-Tech helmet. Evan must have substituted his new gear for the old make-do equipment Bryn was used to playing with. He smiled as he dressed. He felt like a knight of old putting on his suit of armour before a big joust.

This must be what it feels like to be in the Stanley Cup playoffs, Bryn thought as he stepped onto the ice in his new equipment. His helmet and face guard had that new smell and Bryn breathed in the unfamiliar scent.

The ref blew the whistle to signal to the teams that he was ready to drop the first puck. Bryn skated toward the bench and took his place.

He glanced over at the Nighthawks. Their players all looked so big and tough. It was going to be a rough game.

The second the puck hit the ice, it became obvious the ref was going to have his hands full. The Nighthawks were brutal from the start and only got more vicious as the game progressed.

Bryn had picked fast rock tunes to play in his head. The whole team noticed his improved skating and stickhandling. He also moved with an unfamiliar coordination that left him wondering at his own performance.

A couple of times he looked up into the dark stands hoping Evan was watching how well he was doing.

He was skating much better than before, but after a couple of shifts on the ice, Bryn realized even with his tunes going full blast he was no match for the aggressive Nighthawks skaters. Music helped, but it wasn't enough. His lack of hockey skills was painfully obvious.

Up ahead, two Nighthawks forwards were dicing with Zach Lansky, who was valiantly trying to stop them from breaking into the Comets' end.

Bryn was the closest Comet to the action. He gripped his stick harder and headed over to help. He skated in front of the first Nighthawk hoping to take him out of the action so Zach would have the chance to strip the puck from the remaining forward.

"Get out of my way, Speed Bump," Craig Carpenter snarled into Bryn's face.

Bryn recognized him from previous games.

"Make me," he said as he dug his skates into the ice.

Craig cursed and brought the end of his stick-blade up, clipping the edge of Bryn's new helmet.

It wasn't a hard blow, but Bryn hadn't expected it and lost his balance. He heard the ref's shrill whistle as he fell. "That's using your head, Carpenter," Bryn said, wincing. "If I'm not mistaken, that's a four-minute minor for high sticking."

A linesman skated up to Craig, pointing at the penalty box.

Bryn clambered to his feet and headed to the bench for a shift change.

Kelsey, sitting at the end of the players' bench with her clipboard, gave him an encouraging smile. "You okay?" she asked.

Bryn suddenly felt shy at her concern over the minor hit. He reached for a bottle of water. "Sure, with Evan's great new equipment there's no permanent damage..." He saw the look of confusion on Kelsey's face. "I mean *even* this great new equipment isn't permanently damaged." He busied himself taking a long drink of water.

The action was non-stop. Every Comet player was off the bench standing and watching the play. It was near the end of the second period and the score was close. Everyone knew things were going to get bloodier.

The third period saw lots of elbowing, rough checking, and unnecessary slashing. Lucas was amazing.

He had scored six of the Comets' eight goals. He also had a knack of showing up at just the right moment to throw off the Nighthawks' dirty play. A couple of times, Lucas driving off an attack had saved Bryn from kissing the ice.

"Tyler, over here," Lucas called to his left forward,

who was being hemmed in by two Nighthawks. Tyler used a flip pass to get the puck to his teammate. Lucas could take only two strides before he was checked so hard that he was almost knocked off his skates. He lost control of the puck. Jamie Carver hooked it and streaked toward the Comet goal.

Jordan saw him coming and was ready. He slapped the shot down with his trapper and passed it back out to Lucas, who started for the Nighthawks' end.

Before he could get across the blue line, he was tripped and fell to the ice. The Nighthawks recovered the puck and started driving back.

Lucas was still deep in the action when Bryn, switching off with a teammate, came over the boards and raced to join him.

Craig Carpenter was back on the ice. He waited with a grim look on his face as Lucas skated toward the puck handler. Craig nodded his head at Trevor and Jamie who broke away from the men they were covering. All three converged on Lucas.

Bryn, who was further behind the action, saw what was coming. They were going to piledrive Lucas into the boards. This time Lucas was going to be hurt. He tried to catch Lucas to warn him, but he couldn't skate fast enough. He was too slow and Lucas was going to pay for it.

Just then, up ahead, the Nighthawks player with the puck fired a sizzling slapshot right past Jordan and into the net. The goal light whirled around and the whistle blew. Clean goal.

The attack on Lucas broke off and Bryn wondered when they would try again.

★★★

Evan was watching with growing uneasiness as the Nighthawks chased Lucas Coles. He thought of how violent Craig was and how he loved to get revenge. If it weren't for the goal, Lucas would be hurt by now. Evan knew what he had to do. He had to warn the coach. Scrambling down the arena stairs, he headed for the Comets' bench.

"Whoa there, young fella. There's a big game going on and you can't go in there." The security guard blocked his way.

"My brother's playing and I have to get him an important message," Evan pleaded, knowing this was the truth.

"The game's just about over, son, if you wait another few minutes you can tell him then." The kindly guard was just doing his job, but right now Evan needed to get past him.

He took a small plastic flashlight out of his jacket pocket. He held it so only the end of its plastic tube showed. "I have his medicine. He needs it if he's going to play the rest of this game."

"What's your brother's name?" the guard asked.

Evan was getting anxious. He had to warn Lucas what was coming. "Lucas Coles," he lied. "He's the captain of the Comets."

The guard hesitated a moment, then smiled. "Okay, but be quick. I'm not supposed to let any spectators past this point."

Evan nodded and headed for the gate to the Comets bench. The cool air coming off the ice hit his face making him wish he were playing. He spotted Coach Coles standing behind the players' bench. Lucas was waiting near him, ready to go over the boards at the next shift change. Bryn was still on the ice.

"Coach Coles!" Evan yelled, but his voice was drowned out by the crowd cheering a sudden breakaway.

Evan had to get closer, but he knew the security guard was watching him.

"Coach, over here!" He was getting desperate now. There was a break in the play but before he could say anything, Lucas was on the ice and heading for the face-off circle.

Evan shoved the gate open and pushed himself in with the waiting players. "Coach Coles!" He grabbed the coach's sleeve.

The coach frowned. "You're not supposed to be here, son. I can speak to you after the game, but right now, you'd better leave." The man had no idea who Evan was.

"My name is Evan Selkirk and I'm Bryn Selkirk's brother." He saw the disbelieving look on the coach's face. "I have to warn you about the Nighthawks. I used to play for them and I know what Craig Carpenter plans to do to Lucas. You have to stop the game."

"Look, I don't know who you are, but I've known Bryn for several months now and he's never mentioned a brother. You don't even look like him." The coach was looking over at the security guard and Evan knew he had only seconds before he was escorted out.

Kelsey looked up from her stat sheet, frowning. "Bryn doesn't have a brother. I would know," she said confidently.

There was a sudden whoosh of skates and one of the Comets clambered through the gate off the ice. Relief washed over Evan. It was his brother. "Bryn, come over here!"

Bryn was so surprised he stood staring for a moment.

"Hurry up! I'm here to help." Evan shoved his hair out of his eyes. "Tell them who I am."

Bryn looked from Evan to Coach Coles then to Kelsey's shocked face. He took a deep breath. "Evan is my twin brother."

Kelsey's eyebrows shot up at this. "*Twin brother*! You never said anything about a brother."

Bryn cut her off. "Nevermind that now. There's time for explanations later." He turned to Evan. "You said you came to help. How?"

"I'm here to warn you about Craig Carpenter and the Nighthawks. They plan on taking Lucas out in a big way. I'm talking broken bones and worse. You've got to stop them before he's seriously hurt."

"Do you have proof of this, Evan?" Coach Coles asked disbelievingly.

Bryn stepped up and stood beside Evan. "If my brother says it's going to happen, you can believe him."

Just then, a roar went up from the crowd, whistles and shouting followed, then refs and linesmen were moving across the ice fast. A figure lay face down on the ice, unmoving.

16 AND MAY THE BEST TEAM WIN

"Dad! It's Lucas!" Kelsey cried, fear in her voice.

"Oh, man!" Evan cursed with frustration as the other Comets players crowded in front of him to see what had happened. He was too late. They'd done it.

Coach Coles and the paramedic raced toward Lucas's still figure. A ref was bending over him.

Craig Carpenter glided past the Comets bench and smirked at Bryn. "You're next, Speed Bump."

"You can try, Carpenter," Bryn said with what he hoped sounded like rough, tough snake-spit venom. Craig just laughed and skated away.

The whole team watched anxiously as Lucas was attended to.

"What happened?" Bryn asked a linesman who was standing on the ice near their bench.

"We're not sure," the linesman said frowning. "The puck was in the Comets' end so we didn't really see. There was a group of Nighthawks players behind the play in the corner with the Comets' captain. He must have been checked into the boards and fell wrong. The other linesman said there were several Nighthawks players crowding in at the time and his line of sight was screened. It appears to have been an unfortunate accident." He skated away toward the officials' box.

"Unfortunate accident my butt!" Evan said angrily as he pushed through the other Comets players. "That was Craig Carpenter and his gang of thugs for sure. I should have come down here sooner. I knew that jerk would pull something like this."

"Stop blaming yourself, Evan," Bryn said. "It wasn't your fault."

The paramedics brought a stretcher and gently lifted Lucas onto it. His arm was lying at an odd angle.

Coach Coles returned to the Comets' bench. "They're going to take him to the hospital." Lucas's father looked ashen as he watched his son being wheeled away. "I'm sorry I didn't listen to you sooner, Evan. This might have been avoided."

"What happens now, Dad?" Kelsey asked, her clipboard clasped tightly in her arms.

"Lucas wants us to finish the game and that's just what we're going to do. Unfortunately, he left a big hole in the lineup." He looked at his players, deciding who was going to fill in for their fallen captain. Everyone knew that their chances of winning were slim.

Bryn thought a moment. "Evan, you were released from the Nighthawks yesterday, *complete with paperwork.*

The league deadline for signing up new players isn't until tomorrow. That makes you a free agent..."

Evan suddenly started frantically pulling papers out of his jacket. "Got 'em!"

Bryn turned to his coach. "Coach, what if I could get the Comets a really wicked player who was recently released from the Nighthawks?"

The coach appeared confused.

Bryn went on. "Evan is right, I am a second-rate hockey player, but," he added proudly, "a first rate musician." Kelsey gave him another surprised look. "I'll explain later, Kelsey. Right now, we need a top gun to fill in for Lucas. What do you say, Coach? Can we get permission for Evan to play for the Comets on such short notice?"

Coach Coles looked from Evan to Bryn, frowning, "I don't know." Then he glanced over at the Nighthawks bench. "But I'm darn well going to find out," he smiled. "Evan, give me your papers. You and I are going to talk to the officials."

Finally, after what seemed forever, the coach and Evan came back. "After the executives from the Canadian Hockey Association heard how the Nighthawks deliberately hurt Lucas, they were more than happy to sign the paperwork. It is a special case and there are some details to be taken care of later, but as of this minute, Evan is officially a Comet."

"Come on Evan," Bryn said laughing. "You've got

to get dressed in *my* new gear."

When Evan returned he was wearing Bryn's uniform, complete with jersey proudly displaying the name Selkirk and the number 16.

"Welcome to the Comets," Bryn said. He took Evan over to where the rest of the team waited. "Guys, this is my brother Evan and he'll be replacing me for the rest of the game. I think you'll be glad he did." Everyone smiled and nodded at their new teammate.

Evan dropped his visor, which partly hid his face. "Just think of me as Bryn Selkirk—with an attitude."

The crowd cheered and clapped when the Comets took to the ice again. There was only five minutes left in the third period and they needed three goals to win.

The Nighthawks were not expecting the Comets to put up any sort of a fight without their star player. They were totally unprepared for the *Selkirk 16* dynamo who stole the puck and streaked to their net on a fast breakaway. Evan's slapshot was unstoppable and the Comets were suddenly down by only one with four minutes left.

With their new secret weapon, the Comets' defence came alive as they battled for possession of the puck. Using more force than they might have before Lucas was hit, Zach out-muscled Trevor Wells and forced him off the puck. With a quick drop pass, Zach slid the puck to Tyler McBride, who started his run at the net. Evan saw what was happening and took out two Nighthawk players who were zeroing in on Tyler, freeing him for a clear shot.

Paco Jenkins was fast, but fell for Tyler's deke. The goalie's butterfly style of net minding was great until he was on the ice. He was slow to get up. Tyler waited till Paco had committed and was down, then pulled the puck back and fired a hard shot to the top shelf. Bingo! The score was tied.

The Comets hit the ice with the clock ticking down. The crowd was on its feet stamping and cheering.

"One more and we've won, guys," Coach Coles said as the players switched, ready for the next charge. "But even if we don't get that last one, I want you boys to know how proud I am of you. You've played a heck of a hockey game here today."

A mad scramble on the faceoff sent the puck spinning into the Comets' end. Evan was on it in a heartbeat. With a deke any NHL star would have been proud of, he manoeuvred around a crowd of Nighthawks and headed down ice. He was still in the Comets end, but with a clear breakaway all the way to the Nighthawks goal. Suddenly, on his left wing, Craig Carpenter appeared out of nowhere. He moved up next to Evan, but instead of trying to strip the puck from him, he raised his elbow and gave Evan a vicious shot to the head.

The whistle signaled a stoppage of play.

"So much for your breakaway, Speed Bump," Craig growled. Grinning, he turned to Evan. A sudden confused look came over his face as he saw who was smiling back at him.

The ref skated up and took Craig's arm to escort him to the penalty box. "Wait a minute!" Craig protested loudly. "That's not the right guy. Selkirk's not supposed to be on the Comets."

The ref looked at Evan's jersey. "Is your name Selkirk?" he asked.

"You bet, Ref!" Evan said, grinning at Craig.

"And you play for the Comets?" He said matter-of-factly.

"Right again, Ref!" Evan was practically giggling by now.

The ref shook his head. "Come on, Carpenter. You've got two minutes for elbowing."

Craig's face became very red. "I'm telling you, this guy's a ringer!" he shouted into the ref's face. Furious, he shook the ref's arm and gave the official a violent shove, sending the ref spinning away.

The referee skated back and grabbed Craig's arm. "You're done, Carpenter! That just got you a match penalty, and with your record, you can count on more than just a one-game suspension."

Evan heard Craig yelling all the way to the penalty box.

Unfortunately, because this last penalty occurred in the Comets' end, that's where the faceoff was. With only seconds remaining, the Comets had little hope of working the puck all the way to the other end.

If the Nighthawks gained possession on the faceoff this close to the Comets' goal, they would have a real scoring opportunity. Evan groaned when he saw the Nighthawks coach pull their goalie and send in an extra forward.

The three forwards and centre tried to steamroll the Comets on the faceoff, but Evan pushed hard and gained control of the puck. Cursing loudly, Jamie Carver speared Evan, freeing the puck, then slapped it wildly toward the Comets net. The other two Nighthawks forwards broke free and headed after the puck with the Comets right behind.

In a totally unexpected move, Jordan Cairn, the Comets' goalie, skated out of his net toward the crazily careening puck. He pulled his big stick back and slapped the puck with everything he had.

The puck fired past both the Nighthawks and Comets players. It kept going over the centre line and slid past the far blue line. With a satisfying swish, it sunk home into the undefended Nighthawks net just as the final buzzer sounded!

The Comets had won with an end-to-end effort by their sharp-shooting goalie!

The crowd hooted and stamped its feet. Cheering roared around the arena. Evan and the Comets waved to the fans as hats sailed onto the ice. They had done it!

Skating over to the bench, Evan high-fived Bryn.

"*Team Selkirk* rules!" he laughed.

"You and the Comets are going to be a force for the rest of the year, Evan. I look forward to seeing a repeat of today's win at the season championship!" Bryn smiled.

Evan pointed into the noisy crowd cheering in the stands. "Mom and Dad are sitting right over there." Side by side, their arms on each other's shoulders, Evan and Bryn waved at their parents.

17 TRUTH IF YOU DARE

After everyone had changed into their street clothes, the Comets and their parents were gathered in the foyer of the arena waiting to hear word from the hospital about Lucas. Finally Coach Coles came back from the office.

"The doctor says Lucas has a slight concussion and a dislocated shoulder. They're going to keep him in the hospital for observation, so you won't have your captain at the banquet tonight. He says to have a good time and we'll all get together after he's home." Lucas's father looked relieved as he delivered the news.

The players cheered and talk started about a party for Lucas. Everyone was in good spirits as they broke up to leave.

Bryn stood with his family as the news was delivered. He felt a lot better knowing Lucas would be all right.

"Excuse me," Kelsey's voice made Bryn spin around. She looked from Bryn to his brother and finally to his parents. "Aren't you going to introduce me to your *family*, Bryn?" she asked, not smiling. Her voice was icily cool.

"Kelsey!" Bryn said surprised. His throat felt suddenly tight. "Ah, sure. Kelsey Coles, these are my parents, Thomas and Julianne Selkirk, and you know my brother." Bryn noticed again how Evan and his mother's dark looks contrasted so startlingly with Bryn and his dad. It was hard to believe they were in the same family.

"It's very nice to meet you, Mr. and Mrs. Selkirk," Kelsey said formally.

"And it's great to finally meet Bryn's best friend at Westhaven," Julianne Selkirk said warmly.

Kelsey forced a smile. "I'll look forward to seeing you at the banquet tonight."

"Oh, didn't my son tell you?" Bryn's mom said, surprised. "We won't be able to attend the banquet because of Bryn's piano recital in Edmonton, but we'd love to get together when Lucas gets out of the hospital."

"The Edmonton Piano Competition!" Kelsey said, her eyes widening in surprise. "I've heard talk about it at school. I know only the top musicians make it in. I didn't know anyone from Westhaven was going. Bryn never said anything about it." Kelsey stared at Bryn, more hurt in her eyes at this latest news. "Excuse me, I have to go find my dad." She nodded at Bryn's parents then turned and walked quickly away.

"Rats!" Bryn cursed. "Kelsey, wait up. Will you at

least let me explain?" He wasn't sure how he was going to get out of this, but one thing was for sure, he was going to make her listen to the truth. He ran after her. "Will you wait a minute?"

She stopped dead in her tracks then spun on him, furious. "Wait? For what? More lies? Tell me, Bryn, were you ever going to tell me your family secrets? Or am I just a girl you hang out with at school and don't consider a good enough friend to share whole chunks of your life with? You must think I'm an idiot." She was so angry that her voice was shaking. "You know what's the worst part?" Her eyes glinted. *"You didn't trust me."*

She started to turn away again, but Bryn grabbed her arm.

"Let go of me!" she yelled, shaking loose. "I don't ever want to speak to you again, you, you *northern nerd*!"

She ran across the foyer and started out the doors. Bryn didn't know what to do as he watched her go. He turned to walk back to his family and saw Evan striding toward him.

"Are you going to let her get away like this?" he asked.

Bryn was confused. "What can I do? She hates me."

"Did you explain?" his brother asked.

Bryn shook his head. "She never gave me the chance!"

Evan sighed. "She seems like a pretty cool girl, Bryn, and besides, I like a brother who can play hockey, even so-so hockey, and that means you're going to have to practise with me and the Comets to keep your limited skills up. But if you don't get this straightened out with Kelsey, I know you won't come." He spun Bryn around and shoved him in the direction Kelsey had left. "See if you can fix this one little thing on your own."

Bryn nodded at his brother and headed toward the doors.

Kelsey was waiting outside for her family when Bryn caught up with her. He could see she'd been crying and this made him feel worse. "Will you please let me explain? Then if you want you can tell me to get lost, and I will," he asked almost desperately.

She wouldn't look at him, but she nodded her head.

He sighed, knowing how terrible his explanation was going to sound. "I knew you'd be mad at me for lying to you, even though I didn't really lie. I just didn't fill you in on a few things." Nervously, he kept going. "The reason I didn't tell you about Evan and my mom is because my mom is James Bay Cree and after that incident with the van when you were nearly hit, you said you and your family had no use for Indian people." He pressed on. "And when we were walking and the band passed us, you said you didn't like them either. I didn't want you to stop being my friend so I avoided telling you about my family and music. I meant to, but by then so much time had passed, I didn't know how to tell you without looking like an idiot." He looked down at his boots. "Kind of the way I look now."

She didn't say anything and Bryn wasn't sure if she was going to yell at him again or punch him. They waited in silence for several very long minutes.

Kelsey suddenly took a tissue out of her pocket and wiped her eyes. Then she took a deep breath and exhaled loudly. "You idiot," she began in an exasperated tone. "My dad said he didn't like those kids in the van because he knew them from hockey last year and thought they had great potential, which they were throwing away. Instead of working on their hockey, they spend their talent getting into trouble with the law. Bryn, my dad coaches a team from the reserve on weekends. None of my family has any problem with First Nations people."

She shook her head, making her hair bounce. "And as far as music goes, I just didn't like the dumb band *uniforms.* They are so ugly and make the musicians look like geeks. Those feathers in their hats with that gold braid and having to carry your instrument while trying to play decently—don't get me started." She looked at him. "But music, Bryn I *love* real music. I'm in the church choir and if you'd taken the time to ask, I have a pretty good voice." She put her hands in her pockets. "I'm angry because you kept that entire part of your life from me."

Bryn felt like the world's biggest screw-up. "I really am sorry," he said, and meant it.

Kelsey looked at him and her face suddenly softened. "I could have spent all these months being proud of my boyfriend the fantastic pianist, instead of my boyfriend the not-so-great hockey player." She frowned, but the corner of her mouth had the crinkle of a smile starting. "When I think of how I bumped the student who was actually supposed to be your study buddy so I would be next in line…I saw you waiting by the office that first day and I thought you were too cute to waste on Freddie Oldenshaw. Who knew you would be so much trouble?" She swayed toward him and bumped him gently with her shoulder.

Bryn felt his face flush, but he was very pleased. "Okay, I've learned my lesson. Does this mean we're still friends and I can leave for the biggest recital of my life knowing everything's okay?"

She nodded. "Yes, you can leave safely. I wish you the very best of luck. I know you're going to knock their socks off." She looked him directly in the eye. "There is one condition, though."

"Anything," Bryn said gratefully.

"You have to promise never lie to me again or *forget* to tell me important things." Her voice was light, but her eyes said she was serious.

He didn't have to think twice about this one. "I promise. I don't ever want to do that crazy juggling act over again. The truth is much easier for every one."

Kelsey's parents pulled up in a van and waved at her.

She started to leave, then stopped and smiled sheepishly at him. "And Bryn, perhaps when you get back, you could play something just for me." She smiled warmly at him and left.

Bryn felt relieved and excited at the same time. Relieved everything was finally out in the open and excited about tonight's recital. He would never lie to Kelsey again, their friendship was too important. Thinking about the recital reminded him of Mr. Boothby.

A new wave of guilt washed over him as he thought of all the lying that he'd done to his teacher. He owed Mr. Boothby a serious apology. He liked the piano teacher and would explain everything right after the recital. He planned on doing well and that would make apologizing a lot easier. He still had a lot to learn from his teacher.

Evan came through the doors and stood beside his brother, watching the van pull away. "Everything okay?" he asked.

Bryn felt great. Everything had worked out better than he could have imagined. Who knew telling the truth would be the easy way out? He smiled. "I guess you could say that."

"So which of us won the big prize we bet on so long ago?" Evan asked wryly.

Bryn looked thoughtful. "If I remember correctly, the original bet was the winner would be decided by which *team* won the championship. At the time, I was playing for the Comets and you were with the Nighthawks." He nodded his head slowly. "True, I did withdraw for athletic reasons, but my team won the big game, therefore, I win the bet. Simple!"

Evan looked at him out of the corner of his eye. "*Athletic reasons*! You mean you're no athlete, so you quit before they tossed you. As far as being on the winning team, you seem to have forgotten who the newest Comet is and who was on the team at the time of the actual win."

"Do you think we could convince Mom and Dad we need *two* big prizes?" Bryn asked hopefully.

Evan nodded. "If we stick together, you know, *Team Selkirk,* we can do anything."

The brothers looked at each other and grinned conspiratorially as they started back into the building toward their unsuspecting parents.

ACKNOWLEDGEMENTS

I wish to thank Brynley Tourond, and his very knowledgeable father/coach Tim Tourond, for their technical assistance in the writing of this story. Thanks, guys. You are both winners in my book.

The writer wishes to acknowledge Jody Whitney, Director of Education, Tsuu T'ina Nation, and Bob Nicholson, President, Canadian Hockey Association, for their assistance with this project.

MORE SPORTS, MORE ACTION

www.lorimer.ca

CHECK OUT THESE OTHER HOCKEY STORIES FROM LORIMER'S SPORTS STORIES SERIES:

A Goal in Sight

By Jacqueline Guest

Aiden is the toughest defenceman in his Calgary hockey league, often spending as much time in the penalty box as on the ice—and that's the way he likes it. But when he hits another player after a game, Aiden finds himself charged with assault and sentenced to one hundred hours of community service. Unfortunately, Eric, the blind hockey player he's assigned to help, is not exactly what he had in mind...

Hat Trick

By Jacqueline Guest

Leigh is one of the top players on her hockey team, the Falcons—but she's also the only girl and a Métis, and not everyone is happy about that. Soon Leigh's receiving threatening messages, the Falcons' captain tries to get her kicked off the team, and to make matters worse, her mother wants her to perform in a dance recital on the same night as the championship game. When the pressure becomes too intense, Leigh has to face some tough decisions.

Danger Zone

By Michele Martin Bossley

Jason Briggs is the star defenceman on his hockey team, and the toughest checker in the league. But when Jason accidentally checks a player from behind, the boy is seriously hurt. Now the boy's parents want him suspended for good. But how will Jason survive without hockey? Somehow, he must find a way to clear his name—but the odds seem stacked against him.

Deflection!

By Bill Swan

Jake and his two best friends are members of the same league team, the Bear Claws. They may not be "the worst team ever," but there sure is room for improvement—and when they face the Cougars in the city championship, they want to be on top of their game. But personal rivalries and interference from Jake's three all-too-supportive grandfathers start to create tension among the players. Can the Bear Claws get their rhythm back before the big game?

Delaying the Game

By Lorna Schultz Nicholson

All-girls hockey is a whole different world for Kaleigh—there are new teammates, new rules, and new problems to deal with. And when Shane comes along, Kaleigh finds that the world of boys has become just as confusing. Can she stick to her goals and rediscover her love for hockey, or will these distractions throw her off her game for good?

Hockey Night in Transcona

By John Danakas

After years of playing shinny, Cody Powell's dream has come true—he has made it onto the Transcona Sharks, the local league team, and it's finally his time to show everyone what he can do. But when Coach Brackett takes his own son off the front line so that Cody can take his place, Cody has to decide what's more important—taking his time to shine, or sticking up for a friend.

Home Ice

By Beatrice Vandervelde

Determined not to miss the hockey season while staying with relatives in Toronto, Tori signs up to play with the Rangers—the worst team in the league. The only girl on her team, she soon befriends Mary, a girl on a rival team who doesn't think much of hockey. At first, Tori's teammates resent her alliance with the enemy—especially Larry, the Rangers' big, loud first-line centre. But when the team discovers her talent for coaching, things start to look up.

Icebreaker

By Steven Barwin

Greg Stokes can tell you exactly when his life took a turn for the worse. It was the day he and his new stepsister, Amy, joined the same hockey team. Like it wasn't bad enough sharing a house, school, and friends—now they're playing on the same line! Before long, the stepsiblings' game is affected by the deep chill between them. Can they thaw their icy relationship for the sake of the team and their new family?

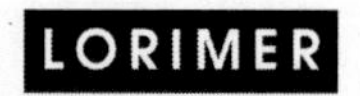

Power Play

By Michele Martin Bossley

In the first game of his first Peewee season, left winger Zach Thomas gets slammed into the boards and knocked out of play with a near season-ending injury. Now he's back on the ice and ready for action—the trouble is, he's off his game because he's afraid of getting hurt. To make matters worse, a bully on an opposing team has decided he has unfinished business to settle with Zach. Can Zach learn how to stand up to his fears—and to the bully?

Roughing

By Lorna Schultz Nicholson

Josh Watson is off to an elite hockey camp for the summer, where he shares a room with Peter Kuiksak, a talented centre from the Northwest Territories. Peter is skilled enough to give Kevin, the star junior player, some serious competition—and Kevin is not exactly happy about that. When Josh learns that Kevin and his friends are planning to pull a dangerous prank on Peter, he must take action before someone gets seriously hurt.

Two Minutes for Roughing

By Joseph Romain

Les Lewchuck loves hockey and plays it every chance he gets, so he's ecstatic when his new friend—a tough-girl goalie named Mickey—invites him to play for a real team, the Metro Cats. He soon finds, however, that Roddy and Lenny Smith, a couple of bullying brothers, run the team and don't take kindly to newcomers. Now Les must find a way to stand up to them before they ruin hockey for him forever.